Ruskin Bond is known for his signature simplistic and witty writing style. He is the author of several bestselling short stories, novellas, collections, essays and children's books; and has contributed a number of poems and articles to various magazines and anthologies. At the age of twenty-three, he won the prestigious John Llewellyn Rhys Prize for his first novel, *The Room on the Roof*. He was also the recipient of the Padma Shri in 1999, Lifetime Achievement Award by the Delhi Government in 2012 and the Padma Bhushan in 2014.

Born in 1934, Ruskin Bond grew up in Jamnagar, Shimla, New Delhi and Dehradun. Apart from three years in the UK, he has spent all his life in India, and now lives in Landour, Mussoorie, with his adopted family.

RUSKIN BOND

Read Well, Write Well

RUPA

Published by
Rupa Publications India Pvt. Ltd 2023
7/16, Ansari Road, Daryaganj
New Delhi 110002

Sales centres:
Bengaluru Chennai
Hyderabad Jaipur Kathmandu
Kolkata Mumbai Prayagraj

This is a work of fiction. Names, characters, places and incidents are either the product of the author's imagination or are used fictitiously and any resemblance to any actual person, living or dead, events or locales is entirely coincidental.

P-ISBN: 978-93-5702-057-2
E-ISBN: 978-93-5702-063-3

Second impression 2024

10 9 8 7 6 5 4 3 2

Printed in India

CONTENTS

INTRODUCTION

Dear students,

'Read well, write well.'

These were my English teacher's words when I was at school, and I took his advice and never regretted it. I have had a long writing life and a good one.

We all want to write well, to have a good command over the language, which is going to take us into and through a successful career, whether it be in science, medicine, technology, economics, journalism, the arts or just plain business! Writing well makes it so much easier to do well in whatever line of work we undertake.

So how do we go about it? How do we choose that mastery over words that is so important to us as we journey from childhood to adulthood?

We read. And we don't read simply in order to be literate. We read in order to be fully educated; to be able to move with confidence in the bigger world; to be knowledgeable; to better understand our fellow humans.

We start early. We start when we are six or seven, as I did when I first opened a book of rhymes and fairy tales and discovered the magic of words. As I grew older, I wanted to create a little magic with my own words, so I began writing poems, stories, essays and letters too. When I applied for a scholarship, it was my well-written letter that won it for me.

This is not a textbook. You have plenty of those in school. This is a selection of some of the things I have written at different times, which I thought would interest young readers and give them enjoyment in the story and in its presentation.

It is so easy to write a boring story that puts you to sleep. That happens when you use too many difficult words and long, complicated sentences. Keep it simple. That's what my teacher told me. Be clear, be exact. Write about people. Write about animals. Write about the world around you. Write about your own life. Write about your dreams.

It's all about words—putting words together in interesting ways. Bringing them to life. That's what I have been doing for over seventy years.

I hope you like some of the things I have written. I hope they help you read more and write better.

My good wishes for your success and happiness.

Your author,
Ruskin Bond

DON'T BE AFRAID OF THE DARK

Don't be afraid of he dark, little one,
The earth must rest when the day is done.
The sun may be harsh, but moonlight—never!
And those stars will be shining forever and ever,
Be friends with the Night, there is nothing to fear,
Just let your thoughts travel to friends far and near.
By day, it does seem that our troubles won't cease,
But at night, late at night, the world is at peace.

GRANNY'S TREE-CLIMBING

Granny was a genius. You'd like to know why?
Because she could climb trees. Spreading or high,
She'd be up their branches in a trice. And mind you,
When last she climbed a tree she was sixty-two.

Ever since childhood, she'd had this gift
For being happier in a tree than in a lift;
And though, as time went by, she would be told
That climbing trees should stop when one grew old—
And that growing old should be gone about gracefully—
She'd laugh and say, 'Well, I'll grow old disgracefully!
I can do it better.' And we had to agree;
For in all the garden there wasn't a tree
She hadn't been up at one time or another—
(Having learned to climb from a loving brother
When she was six)—but it was feared by all
That one day she'd suffer a terrible fall.

The outcome was different—while we were in town
She climbed a tree and couldn't come down!
She remained on her perch until we came home,
We fetched her a ladder, and she came down alone.

As she looked a bit shaken, we sent for our doc,
Who said, 'She is fine—just a bit of a shock.'

He took Granny's temperature. 'Some fever,' he said;
'I strongly recommend a quiet week in bed.'

We sighed with relief and tucked her up well—
Poor Granny! It was just like a season in hell:
Confined to her bedroom, while every breeze
Murmured of summer and dancing leaves...
But she held her peace till she felt stronger,
Then sat up and said, 'I'll lie here no longer!'
She called for my father and told him undaunted
That a house in a tree-top was what she now wanted.
My Dad knew his duty. He said, 'That's all right—
'You'll have what you want—I shall start work tonight.'

With my expert assistance, he soon finished the chore,
Made her a tree-house with windows and a door.
So Granny moved up; and now, everyday,
I go to her room with glasses and a tray.
She sits there in state and drinks cocktails with me,
Upholding her right to reside in a tree.

[Written for Grandmothers' Rights Everywhere]

ROMI AND THE WILDFIRE

I

As Romi was about to mount his bicycle, he saw smoke rising from behind the distant line of trees.

'It looks like a forest fire,' said Prem, his friend and classmate.

'It's well to the east,' said Romi. 'Nowhere near the road.'

'There's a strong wind,' said Prem, looking at the dry leaves swirling across the road.

It was the middle of May, and it hadn't rained in the Terai for several weeks. The grass was brown, the leaves of the trees covered with dust. Even though it was getting on to six o'clock in the evening, the boys' shirts were damp with sweat.

'It will be getting dark soon,' said Prem. 'You'd better spend the night at my house.'

'No, I said I'd be home tonight. My father isn't keeping well. The doctor has given me some tablets for him.'

'You'd better hurry, then. That fire seems to be spreading.'

'Oh, it's far off. It will take me only forty minutes to ride through the forest. 'Bye, Prem—see you tomorrow!'

Romi mounted his bicycle and pedalled off down the main road of the village, scattering stray hens, stray dogs and stray villagers.

'Hey, look where you're going!' shouted an angry villager, leaping out of the way of the oncoming bicycle. 'Do you think you own the road?'

'Of course I own it,' called Romi cheerfully, and cycled on.

His own village lay about seven miles distant, on the other side of the forest; but there was only a primary school in his village, and Romi was now in High School. His father, who was a fairly wealthy sugarcane farmer, had only recently bought him the bicycle. Romi didn't care too much for school and felt there weren't enough holidays; but he enjoyed the long rides, and he got on well with his classmates.

He might have stayed the night with Prem had it not been for the tablets which the Vaid—the village doctor—had given him for his father.

Romi's father was having back trouble, and the medicine had been specially prepared from local herbs.

Having been given such a fine bicycle, Romi felt that the least he could do in return was to get those tablets to his father as early as possible.

He put his head down and rode swiftly out of the village. Ahead of him, the smoke rose from the burning forest and the sky glowed red.

II

He had soon left the village far behind. There was a slight climb, and Romi had to push harder on the pedals to get over the rise. Once over the top, the road went winding down to the edge of the sub-tropical forest.

This was the part Romi enjoyed most. He relaxed, stopped pedalling, and allowed the bicycle to glide gently down the slope. Soon the wind was rushing past him, blowing his hair about his face and making his shirt billow out behind. He burst into song.

A dog from the village ran beside him, barking furiously. Romi shouted to the dog, encouraging him in the race.

Then the road straightened out, and Romi began pedalling again.

The dog, seeing the forest ahead, turned back to the village. It was afraid of the forest.

The smoke was thicker now, and Romi caught the smell of burning timber. But ahead of him the road was clear. He rode on.

It was a rough, dusty road, cut straight through the forest. Tall trees grew on either side, cutting off the last of the daylight. But the spreading glow of the fire on the right lit up the road, and giant tree-shadows danced before the boy on the bicycle.

Usually the road was deserted. This evening it was alive with wild creatures fleeing from the forest fire.

The first animal that Romi saw was a hare, leaping across the road in front of him. It was followed by several more hares. Then a band of monkeys streamed across, chattering excitedly.

They'll be safe on the other side, thought Romi. The fire won't cross the road.

But it was coming closer. And realising this, Romi pedalled harder. In half-an-hour he should be out of the forest.

Suddenly, from the side of the road, several pheasants rose in the air, and with a *whoosh*, flew low across the path, just in front of the oncoming bicycle. Taken by surprise, Romi fell off. When he picked himself up and began brushing his clothes, he saw that his knee was bleeding. It wasn't a deep cut, but he allowed it to bleed a little, took out his handkerchief and bandaged his knee. Then he mounted the bicycle again.

He rode a bit slower now, because birds and animals kept coming out of the bushes.

Not only pheasants but smaller birds, too, were streaming across the road—parrots, jungle crows, owls, magpies—and the air was filled with their cries.

'Everyone's on the move,' thought Romi. It must be a really big fire.

He could see the flames now, reaching out from behind the trees on his right, and he could hear the crackling as the dry leaves caught fire. The air was hot on his face. Leaves, still alight or turning to cinders, floated past.

A herd of deer crossed the road, and Romi had to stop until they had passed. Then he mounted again and rode on; but now, for the first time, he was feeling afraid.

III

From ahead came a faint clanging sound. It wasn't an animal sound, Romi was sure of that. A fire-engine? There were no fire-engines within fifty miles.

The clanging came nearer, and Romi discovered that the noise came from a small boy who was running along the forest path, two milk-cans clattering at his side

'Teju!' called Romi, recognising the boy from a neighbouring village. 'What are you doing out here?'

'Trying to get home, of course,' said Teju, panting along beside the bicycle.

'Jump on,' said Romi, stopping for him.

Teju was only eight or nine—a couple of years younger than Romi. He had come to deliver milk to some road-workers, but the workers had left at the first signs of the fire, and Teju was hurrying home with his cans still full of milk.

He got up on the cross-bar of the bicycle, and Romi moved

on again. He was quite used to carrying friends on the crossbar.

'Keep beating your milk-cans,' said Romi. 'Like that, the animals will know we are coming. My bell doesn't make enough noise. I'm going to get a horn for my cycle!'

'I never knew there were so many animals in the jungle,' said Teju. 'I saw a python in the middle of the road. It stretched right across!'

'What did you do?'

'Just kept running and jumped right over it!'

Teju continued to chatter but Romi's thoughts were on the fire, which was much closer now. Flames shot up from the dry grass and ran up the trunks of trees and along the branches. Smoke billowed out above the forest.

Romi's eyes were smarting and his hair and eyebrows felt scorched. He was feeling tired but he couldn't stop now, he had to get beyond the range of the fire. Another ten or fifteen minutes of steady riding would get them to the small wooden bridge that spanned the little river separating the forest from the sugarcane fields.

Once across the river, they would be safe. The fire could not touch them on the other side, because the forest ended at the river's edge. But could they get to the river in time?

IV

Clang, clang, clang, went Teju's milk-cans. But the sound of the fire grew louder too.

A tall silk-cotton tree, its branches leaning across the road, had caught fire. They were almost beneath it when there was a crash and a burning branch fell to the ground a few yards in front of them.

The boys had to get off the bicycle and leave the road, forcing their way through a tangle of thorny bushes on the left, dragging and pushing at the bicycle and only returning to the road some distance ahead of the burning tree.

'We won't get out in time,' said Teju, back on the cross-bar but feeling disheartened.

'Yes, we will,' said Romi, pedalling with all his might. 'The fire hasn't crossed the road as yet.'

Even as he spoke, he saw a small flame leap up from the grass on the left. It wouldn't be long before more sparks and burning leaves were blown across the road to kindle the grass on the other side.

'Oh, look!' exclaimed Romi, bringing the bicycle to a sudden stop.

'What's wrong now?' asked Teju, rubbing his sore eyes. And then, through the smoke, he saw what was stopping them.

An elephant was standing in the middle of the road.

Teju slipped off the cross-bar, his cans rolling on the ground, bursting open and spilling their contents.

The elephant was about forty feet away. It moved about restlessly, its big ears flapping as it turned its head from side to side, wondering which way to go.

From far to the left, where the forest was still untouched, a herd of elephants moved towards the river. The leader of the herd raised his trunk and trumpeted a call. Hearing it, the elephant in the road raised its own trunk and trumpeted a reply. Then it shambled off into the forest, in the direction of the herd, leaving the way clear.

'Come, Teju, jump on!' urged Romi. 'We can't stay here much longer!'

V

Teju forgot about his milk-cans and pulled himself up on the cross-bar. Romi ran forward with the bicycle, to gain speed, and mounted swiftly. He kept as far as possible to the left of the road, trying to ignore the flames, the crackling, the smoke and the scorching heat.

It seemed that all the animals who could get away had done so. The exodus across the road had stopped.

'We won't stop again,' said Romi, gritting his teeth. 'Not even for an elephant!'

'We're nearly there!' said Teju. He was perking up again.

A jackal, overcome by the heat and smoke, lay in the middle of the path, either dead or unconscious. Romi did not stop. He swerved round the animal. Then he put all his strength into one final effort.

He covered the last hundred yards at top speed, and then they were out of the forest, free-wheeling down the sloping road to the river.

'Look!' shouted Teju. 'The bridge is on fire!'

Burning embers had floated down on to the small wooden bridge, and the dry, ancient timber had quickly caught fire. It was now burning fiercely.

Romi did not hesitate. He left the road, riding the bicycle over sand and pebbles. Then with a rush they went down the river-bank and into the water.

The next thing they knew they were splashing around, trying to find each other in the darkness.

'Help!' cried Teju. 'I'm drowning!'

VI

'Don't be silly,' said Romi. 'The water isn't deep—it's only up to the knees. Come here and grab hold of me.'

Teju splashed across and grabbed Romi by the belt.

'The water's so cold,' he said, his teeth chattering.

'Do you want to go back and warm yourself?' asked Romi. 'Some people are never satisfied. Come on, help me get the bicycle up. It's down here, just where we are standing.'

Together they managed to heave the bicycle out of the water and stand it upright.

'Now sit on it,' said Romi. 'I'll push you across.'

'We'll be swept away,' said Teju.

'No, we won't. There's not much water in the river at this time of the year. But the current is quite strong in the middle, so sit still. All right?'

'All right,' said Teju nervously.

Romi began guiding the bicycle across the river, one hand on the seat and one hand on the handlebar. The river was shallow and sluggish in midsummer; even so, it was quite swift in the middle. But having got safely out of the burning forest, Romi was in no mood to let a little river defeat him.

He kicked off his shoes, knowing they would be lost; and then gripping the smooth stones of the river-bed with his toes, he concentrated on keeping his balance and getting the bicycle and Teju through the middle of the stream. The water here came up to his waist, and the current would have been too strong for Teju. But when they reached the shallows, Teju got down and helped Romi push the bicycle.

They reached the opposite bank, and sank down on the grass.

'We can rest now,' said Romi. 'But not all night – I've got

some medicine to give to my father.' He felt in his pockets and found that the tablets in their envelope, had turned into a soggy mess. 'Oh well, he had to take them with water anyway,' he said.

They watched the fire as it continued to spread through the forest. It had crossed the road down which they had come. The sky was a bright red, and the river reflected the colour of the sky.

Several elephants had found their way down to the river. They were cooling off by spraying water on each other with their trunks. Further downstream there were deer and other animals.

Romi and Teju looked at each other in the glow from the fire. They hadn't known each other very well before. But now they felt they had been friends for years.

'What are you thinking about?' asked Teju.

'I'm thinking,' said Romi, 'that even if the fire is out in a day or two, it will be a long time before the bridge is repaired. So it will be a nice long holiday from school!'

'But you can walk across the river,' said Teju. 'You just did it.'

'Impossible,' said Romi. 'It's much too swift.'

A LONG WALK FOR BINA

I

A leopard, lithe and sinewy, drank at the mountain stream, and then lay down on the grass to bask in the late February sunshine. Its tail twitched occasionally and the animal appeared to be sleeping. At the sound of distant voices it raised its head to listen, then stood up and leapt lightly over the boulders in the stream, disappearing among the trees on the opposite bank.

A minute or two later, three children came walking down the forest path. They were a girl and two boys, and they were singing in their local dialect an old song they had learnt from their grandparents.

> Five more miles to go!
> We climb through rain and snow.
> A river to cross...
> A mountain to pass...
> Now we've four more miles to go!

Their school satchels looked new, their clothes had been washed and pressed. Their loud and cheerful singing startled a spotted forktail. The bird left its favourite rock in the stream and flew down the dark ravine.

'Well, we have only three more miles to go,' said the bigger boy, Prakash, who had been this way hundreds of times. 'But first we have to cross the stream.'

He was a sturdy twelve-year-old with eyes like black currants and a mop of bushy hair that refused to settle down on his head. The girl and her small brother were taking this path for the first time.

'I'm feeling tired, Bina,' said the little boy.

Bina smiled at him, and Prakash said, 'Don't worry, Sonu, you'll get used to the walk. There's plenty of time.' He glanced at the old watch he'd been given by his grandfather. It needed constant winding. 'We can rest here for five or six minutes.'

They sat down on a smooth boulder and watched the clear water of the shallow stream tumbling downhill. Bina examined the old watch on Prakash's wrist. The glass was badly scratched and she could barely make out the figures on the dial. 'Are you sure it still gives the right time?' she asked.

'Well, it loses five minutes every day, so I put it ten minutes ahead at night. That means by morning it's quite accurate! Even our teacher, Mr Mani, asks me for the time. If he doesn't ask, I tell him! The clock in our classroom keeps stopping.'

They removed their shoes and let the cold mountain water run over their feet. Bina was the same age as Prakash. She had pink cheeks, soft brown eyes, and hair that was just beginning to lose its natural curls. Hers was a gentle face, but a determined little chin showed that she could be a strong person. Sonu, her younger brother, was ten. He was a thin boy who had been sickly as a child but was now beginning to fill out. Although he did not look very athletic, he could run like the wind.

II

Bina had been going to school in her own village of Koli, on the other side of the mountain. But it had been a primary school, finishing at Class 5. Now, in order to study in Class 6, she would have to walk several miles every day to Nauti, where there was a high school going up to Class 8. It had been decided that Sonu would also shift to the new school, to give Bina company. Prakash, their neighbour in Koli, was already a pupil at the Nauti school. His mischievous nature, which sometimes got him into trouble, had resulted in him having to repeat a year.

But this didn't seem to bother him. 'What's the hurry?' he had told his indignant parents. 'You're not sending me to a foreign land when I finish school. And our cows aren't running away, are they?'

'You would prefer to look after the cows, wouldn't you?' asked Bina, as they got up to continue their walk.

'Oh, school's all right. Wait till you see old Mr Mani. He always gets our names mixed up, as well as the subjects he's supposed to be teaching. At our last lesson, instead of maths, he gave us a geography lesson!'

'More fun than maths,' said Bina.

'Yes, but there's a new teacher this year. She's very young they say, just out of college. I wonder what she'll be like.'

Bina walked faster and Sonu had some trouble keeping up with them. She was excited about the new school and the prospect of different surroundings. She had seldom been outside her own village, with its small school and single ration shop. The day's routine never varied—helping her mother in the fields or with household tasks like fetching water from the spring or cutting grass and fodder for the cattle. Her father, who was a soldier, was away for nine months in the year and Sonu was still too small for the heavier tasks.

As they neared Nauti Village, they were joined by other

children coming from different directions. Even where there were no major roads, the mountains were full of little lanes and shortcuts. Like a game of snakes and ladders, these narrow paths zigzagged around the hills and villages, cutting through fields and crossing narrow ravines until they came together to form a fairly busy road along which mules, cattle and goats joined the throng.

Nauti was a fairly large village, and from here a broader but dustier road started for Tehri. There was a small bus, several trucks and (for part of the way) a road roller. The road hadn't been completed because the heavy diesel roller couldn't take the steep climb to Nauti. It stood on the roadside halfway up the road from Tehri.

Prakash knew almost everyone in the area, and exchanged greetings and gossip with other children as well as with muleteers, bus drivers, milkmen and labourers working on the road. He loved telling everyone the time, even if they weren't interested.

'It's nine o'clock,' he would announce, glancing at his wrist. 'Isn't your bus leaving today?'

'Off with you!' the bus driver would respond, 'I'll leave when I'm ready.'

As the children approached Nauti, the small flat school buildings came into view on the outskirts of the village, fringed by a line of long-leaved pines. A small crowd had assembled on the one playing field. Something unusual seemed to have happened. Prakash ran forward to see what it was all about. Bina and Sonu stood aside, waiting in a patch of sunlight near the boundary wall.

Prakash soon came running back to them. He was bubbling over with excitement.

'It's Mr Mani!' he gasped. 'He's disappeared! People are saying a leopard must have carried him off!'

III

Mr Mani wasn't really old. He was about fifty-five and was expected to retire soon. But for the children, most adults over forty seemed ancient! And Mr Mani had always been a bit absent-minded, even as a young man.

He had gone out for his early morning walk, saying he'd be back by eight o'clock, in time to have his breakfast and be ready for class. He wasn't married, but his sister and her husband stayed with him. When it was past nine o'clock, his sister presumed he'd stopped at a neighbour's house for breakfast (he loved tucking into other people's breakfast) and that he had gone on to school from there. But when the school bell rang at ten o'clock, and everyone but Mr Mani was present, questions were asked and guesses were made.

No one had seen him return from his walk and enquiries made in the village showed that he had not stopped at anyone's house. For Mr Mani to disappear was puzzling; for him to disappear without his breakfast was extraordinary.

Then a milkman returning from the next village said he had seen a leopard sitting on a rock on the outskirts of the pine forest. There had been talk of a cattle-killer in the valley, of leopards and other animals being displaced by the construction of a dam. But as yet no one had heard of a leopard attacking a man. Could Mr Mani have been its first victim? Someone found a strip of red cloth entangled in a blackberry bush and went running through the village showing it to everyone. Mr Mani had been known to wear red pyjamas. Surely he had been seized and eaten! But where were his remains? And why had he been in his pyjamas?

Meanwhile, Bina and Sonu and the rest of the children had

followed their teachers into the school playground. Feeling a little lost, Bina looked around for Prakash. She found herself facing a dark, slender young woman wearing spectacles, who must have been in her early twenties—just a little too old to be another student. She had a kind, expressive face and she seemed a little concerned by all that had been happening.

Bina noticed that she had lovely hands; it was obvious that the new teacher hadn't milked cows or worked in the fields!

'You must be new here,' said the teacher, smiling at Bina. 'And is this your little brother?'

'Yes, we've come from Koli Village. We were at school there.'

'It's a long walk from Koli. You didn't see any leopards, did you? Well, I'm new too. Are you in the Class 6?'

'Sonu is in the third. I'm in the 6th.'

'Then I'm your new teacher. My name is Tania Ramola. Come along, let's see if we can settle down in our classroom.'

◆

Mr Mani turned up at twelve o'clock, wondering what all the fuss was about. No, he snapped, he had not been attacked by a leopard; and yes, he had lost his pyjamas and would someone kindly return them to him?

'How did you lose your pyjamas, sir?' asked Prakash.

'They were blown off the washing line!' snapped Mr Mani.

After much questioning, Mr Mani admitted that he had gone further than he had intended, and that he had lost his way coming back. He had been a bit upset because the new teacher, a slip of a girl, had been given charge of the 6th, while he was still with the 5th, along with that troublesome boy Prakash, who kept on reminding him of the time! The Headmaster had explained that as Mr Mani was due to retire at the end of the year, the school did not wish to burden him with a senior class. But Mr Mani looked upon the whole thing as a plot to get rid of him. He glowered at Miss Ramola whenever he passed her. And when she smiled back at him, he looked the other way!

Mr Mani had been getting even more absent-minded of late—putting on his shoes without his socks, wearing his homespun waistcoat inside out, mixing up people's names and, of course, eating other people's lunches and dinners. His sister had made a mutton broth for the postmaster, who was down with 'flu', and had asked Mr Mani to take it over in a thermos. When the postmaster opened the thermos, he found only a few drops of broth at the bottom—Mr Mani had drunk the rest somewhere along the way.

When sometimes Mr Mani spoke of his coming retirement, it was to describe his plans for the small field he owned just behind the house. Right now, it was full of potatoes, which did not require much looking after; but he had plans for growing dahlias, roses, French beans, and other fruits and flowers.

The next time he visited Tehri, he promised himself, he would buy some dahlia bulbs and rose cuttings. The monsoon season would be a good time to put them down. And meanwhile, his potatoes were still flourishing.

IV

Bina enjoyed her first day at the new school. She felt at ease with Miss Ramola, as did most of the boys and girls in her class. Tania Ramola had been to distant towns such as Delhi and Lucknow—places they had only heard about—and it was said that she had a brother who was a pilot and flew planes all over the world. Perhaps he'd fly over Nauti some day!

Most of the children had of course seen planes flying overhead, but none of them had seen a ship, and only a few had been on a train. Tehri mountain was far from the railway and hundreds of miles from the sea. But they all knew about the big dam that was being built at Tehri, just forty miles away.

Bina, Sonu and Prakash had company for part of the way home, but gradually the other children went off in different directions. Once they had crossed the stream, they were on their own again.

It was a steep climb all the way back to their village. Prakash had a supply of peanuts which he shared with Bina and Sonu, and at a small spring they quenched their thirst.

When they were less than a mile from home, they met a postman who had finished his round of the villages in the area and was now returning to Nauti.

'Don't waste time along the way,' he told them. 'Try to get home before dark.'

'What's the hurry?' asked Prakash, glancing at his watch. 'It's only five o'clock.'

'There's a leopard around. I saw it this morning, not far from the stream. No one is sure how it got here. So don't take any chances. Get home early.'

'So, there really is a leopard,' said Sonu.

They took his advice and walked faster, and Sonu forgot to complain about his aching feet.

They were home well before sunset.

There was a smell of cooking in the air and they were hungry.

'Cabbage and roti,' said Prakash gloomily. 'But I could eat anything today.' He stopped outside his small slate-roofed house, and Bina and Sonu waved goodbye and carried on across a couple of ploughed fields until they reached their small stone house.

'Stuffed tomatoes,' said Sonu, sniffing just outside the front door.

'And lemon pickle,' said Bina, who had helped cut, sun and salt the lemons a month previously.

Their mother was lighting the kitchen stove. They greeted her with great hugs and demands for an immediate dinner. She was a good cook who could make even the simplest of dishes taste delicious. Her favourite saying was, 'Home-made bread is better than roast meat abroad,' and Bina and Sonu had to agree.

Electricity had yet to reach their village, and they took their meal by the light of a kerosene lamp. After the meal, Sonu settled down to do a little homework, while Bina stepped outside to look at the stars.

Across the fields, someone was playing a flute. 'It must be Prakash,' thought Bina. 'He always breaks off on the high notes.' But the flute music was simple and appealing, and she began singing softly to herself in the dark.

V

Mr Mani was having trouble with the porcupines. They had been getting into his garden at night and digging up and eating his potatoes. From his bedroom window—left open now that the mild April weather had arrived—he could listen to them enjoying the vegetables he had worked hard to grow. Scrunch, scrunch! *katar, katar*, as their sharp teeth sliced through the largest and juiciest of potatoes. For Mr Mani it was as though they were biting through his own flesh. And the sound of them digging industriously as they rooted up those healthy, leafy plants made him tremble with rage and indignation. The unfairness of it all!

Yes, Mr Mani hated porcupines. He prayed for their destruction, their removal from the face of the earth. But, as his friends were quick to point out, 'The creator made porcupines too,' and in any case you could never see the creatures or catch them, they were completely nocturnal.

Mr Mani got out of bed every night, torch in one hand, a stout stick in the other but, as soon as he stepped into the garden, the crunching and digging stopped and he was greeted by the most infuriating of silences. He would grope around in the dark, swinging wildly with the stick, but not a single porcupine was to be seen or heard. As soon as he was back in bed, the sounds would start all over again—scrunch, scrunch, *katar, katar*...

Mr Mani came to his class tired and dishevelled, with rings under his eyes and a permanent frown on his face. It took some time for his pupils to discover the reason for his misery, but when they did, they felt sorry for their teacher and took to discussing ways and means of saving his potatoes from the porcupines.

It was Prakash who came up with the idea of a moat or water ditch. 'Porcupines don't like water,' he said knowledgeably.

'How do you know?' asked one of his friends.

'Throw water on one and see how it runs! They don't like getting their quills wet.'

There was no one who could disprove Prakash's theory, and the class fell in with the idea of building a moat, especially as it meant getting most of the day off.

'Anything to make Mr Mani happy,' said the Headmaster, and the rest of the school watched with envy as the pupils of Class 5, armed with spades and shovels collected from all parts of the village, took up their positions around Mr Mani's potato field and began digging a ditch.

By evening the moat was ready, but it was still dry and the porcupines got in again that night and had a great feast.

'At this rate,' said Mr Mani gloomily, 'there won't be any potatoes left to save.'

But the next day, Prakash and the other boys and girls managed to divert the water from a stream that flowed past the village. They had the satisfaction of watching it flow gently into the ditch. Everyone went home in a good mood. By nightfall, the ditch had overflowed, the potato field was flooded, and Mr Mani found himself trapped inside his house. But Prakash and his friends had won the day. The porcupines stayed away that night!

◆

A month had passed, and wild violets, daisies and buttercups now sprinkled the hill slopes and, on her way to school, Bina gathered enough to make a little posy. The bunch of flowers fitted easily into an old ink well. Miss Ramola was delighted to find this little display in the middle of her desk.

'Who put these here?' she asked in surprise.

Bina kept quiet, and the rest of the class smiled secretively. After that, they took turns bringing flowers for the classroom.

On her long walks to school and home again, Bina became aware that April was the month of new leaves. The oak leaves were bright green above and silver beneath, and when they rippled in the breeze, they were clouds of silvery green. The path was strewn with old leaves, dry and crackly. Sonu loved kicking them around.

Clouds of white butterflies floated across the stream. Sonu was chasing a butterfly when he stumbled over something dark and repulsive. He went sprawling on the grass. When he got to his feet, he looked down at the remains of a small animal.

'Bina! Prakash! Come quickly!' he shouted.

It was part of a sheep, killed some days earlier by a much larger animal.

'Only a leopard could have done this,' said Prakash.

'Let's get away, then,' said Sonu. 'It might still be around!'

'No, there's nothing left to eat. The leopard will be hunting elsewhere by now. Perhaps it's moved on to the next valley.'

'Still, I'm frightened,' said Sonu. 'There may be more leopards!'

Bina took him by the hand. 'Leopards don't attack humans!' she said.

'They will, if they get a taste for people!' insisted Prakash.

'Well, this one hasn't attacked any people as yet,' said Bina, although she couldn't be sure. Hadn't there been rumours of a leopard attacking some workers near the dam? But she did not want Sonu to feel afraid, so she did not mention the story. All she said was, 'It has probably come here because of all the activity near the dam.'

All the same, they hurried home. And for a few days, whenever they reached the stream, they crossed over very quickly, unwilling to linger too long at that lovely spot.

VI

A few days later, a school party was on its way to Tehri to see the new dam that was being built.

Miss Ramola had arranged to take her class, and Mr Mani, not wishing to be left out, insisted on taking his class as well. That meant there were about fifty boys and girls taking part in the outing. The little bus could only take thirty. A friendly truck driver agreed to take some children if they were prepared to sit on sacks of potatoes. And Prakash persuaded the owner of the diesel roller to turn it around and head it back to Tehri—with him and a couple of friends up on the driving seat.

Prakash's small group set off at sunrise, as they had to walk some distance in order to reach the stranded road roller. The bus left at 9 a.m. with Miss Ramola and her class, and Mr Mani and some of his pupils. The truck was to follow later.

It was Bina's first visit to a large town, and her first bus ride.

The sharp curves along the winding, downhill road made several children feel sick. The bus driver seemed to be in a tearing hurry. He took them along at a rolling, rollicking speed, which made Bina feel quite giddy. She rested her head on her arms and refused to look out of the window. Hairpin bends and cliff edges, pine forests and snow-capped peaks, all swept past her, but she felt too ill to want to look at anything. It was just as well—those sudden drops, hundreds of feet to the valley below, were quite frightening. Bina began to wish that she hadn't come—or that she had joined Prakash on the road roller instead!

Miss Ramola and Mr Mani didn't seem to notice the lurching and groaning of the old bus. They had made this journey many times. They were busy arguing about the advantages and disadvantages of large dams—an argument that was to continue on and off for much of the day.

Meanwhile, Prakash and his friends had reached the roller. The driver hadn't turned up, but they managed to reverse it and get it going in the direction of Tehri. They were soon overtaken by both bus and truck but kept moving along at a steady chug. Prakash spotted Bina at the window of the bus and waved cheerfully. She responded feebly.

Bina felt better when the road levelled out near Tehri. As they crossed an old bridge over the wide river, they were startled by a loud bang which made the bus shudder. A cloud of dust rose above the town.

'They're blasting the mountain,' said Miss Ramola.

'End of a mountain,' said Mr Mani, mournfully.

While they were drinking cups of tea at the bus stop, waiting for the potato truck and the road roller, Miss Ramola and Mr Mani continued their argument about the dam. Miss Ramola maintained that it would bring electric power and water for irrigation to large areas of the country, including the surrounding area. Mr Mani declared that it was a menace, as it was situated in an earthquake zone. There would be a terrible disaster if the dam burst! Bina found it all very confusing. And what about the animals in the area, she wondered, what would happen to them?

The argument was becoming quite heated when the potato truck arrived. There was no sign of the road roller, so it was decided that Mr Mani should wait for Prakash and his friends while Miss Ramola's group went ahead.

◆

Some eight or nine miles before Tehri, the road roller had broken down, and Prakash and his friends were forced to walk. They had not gone far, however, when a mule train came along—five or six mules that had been delivering sacks of grain in Nauti. A boy rode on the first mule, but the others had no load.

'Can you give us a ride to Tehri?' called Prakash.

'Make yourselves comfortable,' said the boy.

There were no saddles, only gunny sacks strapped on to the mules with rope. They had a rough but jolly ride down to the Tehri bus stop. None of them had ever ridden mules; but they had saved at least an hour on the road.

Looking around the bus stop for the rest of the party, they could find no one from their school. And Mr Mani, who should have been waiting for them, had vanished.

VII

Tania Ramola and her group had taken the steep road to the hill above Tehri. Half an hour's climbing brought them to a little plateau which overlooked the town, the river and the dam site.

The earthworks for the dam were only just coming up, but a wide tunnel had been bored through the mountain to divert the river into another channel. Down below, the old town was still spread out across the valley and from a distance it looked quite charming and picturesque.

'Will the whole town be swallowed up by the waters of the dam?' asked Bina.

'Yes, all of it,' said Miss Ramola. 'The clock tower and the old palace. The long bazaar, and the temples, the schools and the jail, and hundreds of houses, for many miles up the valley. All those people will have to go—thousands of them! Of course they'll be resettled elsewhere.'

'But the town's been here for hundreds of years,' said Bina. 'They were quite happy without the dam, weren't they?'

'I suppose they were. But the dam isn't just for them—it's for the millions who live further downstream, across the plains.'

'And it doesn't matter what happens to this place?'

'The local people will be given new homes somewhere else.' Miss Ramola found herself on the defensive and decided to change the subject. 'Everyone must be hungry. It's time we had our lunch.'

Bina kept quiet. She didn't think the local people would want to go away. And it was a good thing, she mused, that there was only a small stream and not a big river running past her village. To be uprooted like this—a town and hundreds of villages—and put down somewhere on the hot, dusty plains—seemed to her unbearable.

'Well, I'm glad I don't live in Tehri,' she said.

She did not know it, but all the animals and most of the birds had already left the area. The leopard had been among them.

◆

They walked through the colourful, crowded bazaar, where fruit sellers did business beside silversmiths, and pavement vendors sold everything from umbrellas to glass bangles. Sparrows attacked sacks of grain, monkeys made off with bananas, and stray cows and dogs rummaged in refuse bins, but nobody took any notice. Music blared from radios. Buses blew their horns. Sonu bought a whistle to add to the general din, but Miss Ramola told him to put it away. Bina had kept five rupees aside, and now she used it to buy a cotton headscarf for her mother.

As they were about to enter a small restaurant for a meal, they were joined by Prakash and his companions; but of Mr Mani there was still no sign.

'He must have met one of his relatives,' said Prakash. 'He has relatives everywhere.'

After a simple meal of rice and lentils, they walked the length of the bazaar without finding Mr Mani. At last, when they were about to give up the search, they saw him emerge from a by-lane, a large sack slung over his shoulder.

'Sir, where have you been?' asked Prakash. 'We have been looking for you everywhere.'

On Mr Mani's face was a look of triumph.

'Help me with this bag,' he said breathlessly.

'You've bought more potatoes, sir,' said Prakash.

'Not potatoes, boy. Dahlia bulbs!'

VIII

It was dark by the time they were all back in Nauti. Mr Mani had refused to be separated from his sack of dahlia bulbs, and had been forced to sit in the back of the truck with Prakash and most of the boys.

Bina did not feel so ill on the return journey. Going uphill was definitely better than going downhill! But by the time the bus reached Nauti it was too late for most of the children to walk back to the more distant villages. The boys were put up in different homes, while the girls were given beds in the school verandah.

The night was warm and still. Large moths fluttered around the single bulb that lit the verandah. Counting moths, Sonu soon fell asleep. But Bina stayed awake for some time, listening to the sounds of the night. A nightjar went tonk-tonk in the bushes, and somewhere in the forest an owl hooted softly. The sharp call of a barking deer travelled up the valley from the direction of the stream. Jackals kept howling. It seemed that there were more of them than ever before.

Bina was not the only one to hear the barking deer. The leopard, stretched full length on a rocky ledge, heard it too. The leopard raised its head and then got up slowly. The deer was its natural prey. But there weren't many left, and that was why the leopard, robbed of its forest by the dam, had taken to attacking dogs and cattle near the villages.

As the cry of the barking deer sounded nearer, the leopard left its lookout point and moved swiftly through the shadows towards the stream.

IX

In early June, the hills were dry and dusty, and forest fires broke out, destroying shrubs and trees, killing birds and small animals. The resin in the pines made these trees burn more fiercely, and the wind would take sparks from the trees and carry them into the dry grass and leaves, so that new fires would spring up before the old ones had died out. Fortunately, Bina's village was not in the pine belt; the fires did not reach it. But Nauti was surrounded by a fire that raged for three days, and the children had to stay away from school.

And then, towards the end of June, the monsoon rains arrived and there was an end to forest fires. The monsoon lasts three months and the lower Himalayas would be drenched in rain, mist and cloud for the next three months.

The first rain arrived while Bina, Prakash and Sonu were returning home from school. Those first few drops on the dusty path made them cry out with excitement. Then the rain grew heavier and a wonderful aroma rose from the earth.

'The best smell in the world!' exclaimed Bina.

Everything suddenly came to life. The grass, the crops, the trees, the birds. Even the leaves of the trees glistened and looked new.

That first wet weekend, Bina and Sonu helped their mother plant beans, maize and cucumbers. Sometimes, when the rain was very heavy, they had to run indoors. Otherwise they worked in the rain, the soft mud clinging to their bare legs.

Prakash now owned a dog, a black dog with one ear up and one ear down. The dog ran around getting in everyone's way, barking at cows, goats, hens and humans, without frightening any of them. Prakash said it was a very clever dog, but no one else seemed to think so. Prakash also said it would protect the village from the leopard, but others said the dog would be the first to be taken—he'd run straight into the jaws of Mr Spots!

In Nauti, Tania Ramola was trying to find a dry spot in the quarters she'd been given. It was an old building and the roof was leaking in several places. Mugs and buckets were scattered about the floor in order to catch the drips.

Mr Mani had dug up all his potatoes and presented them to the friends and neighbours who had given him lunches and dinners. He was having the time of his life, planting dahlia bulbs all over his garden.

'I'll have a field of many-coloured dahlias!' he announced. 'Just wait till the end of August!'

'Watch out for those porcupines,' warned his sister. 'They eat dahlia bulbs too!'

Mr Mani made an inspection tour of his moat, no longer in flood, and found everything in good order. Prakash had done his job well.

◆

Now, when the children crossed the stream, they found that the water level had risen by about a foot. Small cascades had turned into waterfalls. Ferns had sprung up on the banks. Frogs chanted.

Prakash and his dog dashed across the stream. Bina and Sonu followed more cautiously. The current was much stronger now and the water was almost up to their knees. Once they had crossed the stream, they hurried along the path, anxious not to be caught in a sudden downpour.

By the time they reached school, each of them had two or three leeches clinging to their legs. They had to use salt to remove them. The leeches were the most troublesome part of the rainy season. Even the leopard did not like them. It could not lie in the long grass without getting leeches on its paws and face.

One day, when Bina, Prakash and Sonu were about to cross the stream they heard a low rumble, which grew louder every second. Looking up at the opposite hill, they saw several trees shudder, tilt outwards and begin to fall. Earth and rocks bulged out from the mountain, then came crashing down into the ravine.

'Landslide!' shouted Sonu.

'It's carried away the path,' said Bina. 'Don't go any further.'

There was a tremendous roar as more rocks, trees and bushes fell away and crashed down the hillside.

Prakash's dog, who had gone ahead, came running back, tail between his legs.

They remained rooted to the spot until the rocks had stopped falling and the dust had settled. Birds circled the area, calling wildly. A frightened barking deer ran past them.

'We can't go to school now,' said Prakash. 'There's no way around.'

They turned and trudged home through the gathering mist.

In Koli, Prakash's parents had heard the roar of the landslide. They were setting out in search of the children when they saw them emerge from the mist, waving cheerfully.

X

They had to miss school for another three days, and Bina was afraid they might not be able to take their final exams. Although Prakash was not really troubled at the thought of missing exams, he did not like feeling helpless just because their path had been swept away. So he explored the hillside until he found a goat-track going around the mountain. It joined up with another path near Nauti. This made their walk longer by a mile, but Bina did not mind. It was much cooler now that the rains were in full swing.

The only trouble with the new route was that it passed close to the leopard's lair. The animal had made this area its own since being forced to leave the dam area.

One day Prakash's dog ran ahead of them barking furiously. Then he ran back whimpering.

'He's always running away from something,' observed Sonu. But a minute later he understood the reason for the dog's fear.

They rounded a bend and Sonu saw the leopard standing in their way. They were struck dumb—too terrified to run. It was a strong, sinewy creature. A low growl rose from its throat. It seemed ready to spring.

They stood perfectly still, afraid to move or say a word. And the leopard must have been equally surprised. It stared at them for a few seconds, then bounded across the path and into the oak forest.

Sonu was shaking. Bina could hear her heart hammering. Prakash could only stammer: 'Did you see the way he sprang? Wasn't he beautiful?'

He forgot to look at his watch for the rest of the day.

A few days later, Sonu stopped and pointed to a large outcrop of rock on the next hill.

The leopard stood far above them, outlined against the sky. It looked strong, majestic. Standing beside it were two young cubs.

'Look at those little ones!' exclaimed Sonu.

'So it's a female, not a male,' said Prakash.

'That's why she was killing so often,' said Bina. 'She had to feed her cubs too.'

They remained still for several minutes, gazing up at the leopard and her cubs. The leopard family took no notice of them.

'She knows we are here,' said Prakash, 'but she doesn't care. She knows we won't harm them.'

'We are cubs too!' said Sonu.

'Yes,' said Bina. 'And there's still plenty of space for all of us. Even when the dam is ready there will still be room for leopards and humans.'

XI

The school exams were over. The rains were nearly over too. The landslide had been cleared, and Bina, Prakash and Sonu were once again crossing the stream.

There was a chill in the air, for it was the end of September.

Prakash had learnt to play the flute quite well, and he played on the way to school and then again on the way home. As a result he did not look at his watch so often. One morning they found a small crowd in front of Mr Mani's house.

'What could have happened?' wondered Bina. 'I hope he hasn't got lost again.'

'Maybe he's sick,' said Sonu.

'Maybe it's the porcupines,' said Prakash.

But it was none of these things.

Mr Mani's first dahlia was in bloom, and half the village

had turned up to look at it! It was a huge red double dahlia, so heavy that it had to be supported with sticks. No one had ever seen such a magnificent flower!

Mr Mani was a happy man. And his mood only improved over the coming week, as more and more dahlias flowered—crimson, yellow, purple, mauve, white—button dahlias, pom-pom dahlias, spotted dahlias, striped dahlias... Mr Mani had them all! A dahlia even turned up on Tania Ramola's desk—he got along quite well with her now—and another brightened up the Headmaster's study.

A week later, on their way home—it was almost the last day of the school term—Bina, Prakash and Sonu talked about what they might do when they grew up.

'I think I'll become a teacher,' said Bina. 'I'll teach children about animals and birds, and trees and flowers.'

'Better than maths!' said Prakash.

'I'll be a pilot,' said Sonu. 'I want to fly a plane like Miss Ramola's brother.'

'And what about you, Prakash?' asked Bina.

Prakash just smiled and said, 'Maybe I'll be a flute player,' and he put the flute to his lips and played a sweet melody.

'Well, the world needs flute players too,' said Bina, as they fell into step beside him.

The leopard had been stalking a barking deer. She paused when she heard the flute and the voices of the children. Her own young ones were growing quickly, but the girl and the two boys did not look much older.

They had started singing their favourite song again.

Five more miles to go!
We climb through rain and snow,

A river to cross…
A mountain to pass…
Now we've four more miles to go!

The leopard waited until they had passed, before returning to the trail of the barking deer.

THE HARE IN THE MOON

A long time ago, when animals could talk, there lived in a forest four wise creatures—a hare, a jackal, an otter and a monkey.

They were good friends, and every evening they would sit together in a forest glade to discuss the events of the day, exchange advice, and make good resolutions. The hare was the noblest and wisest of the four. He believed in the superiority of men and women, and was always telling his friends tales of human goodness and wisdom.

One evening, when the moon rose in the sky—and in those days the moon's face was clear and unmarked—the hare looked up at it carefully and said: 'Tomorrow good men will observe a fast, for I can see that it will be the middle of the month. They will eat no food before sunset, and during the day they will give alms to any beggar or holy man who may meet them. Let us promise to do the same. In that way, we can come a little closer to human beings in dignity and wisdom.'

The others agreed, and then went their different ways.

Next day, the otter got up, stretched himself, and was preparing to get his breakfast when he remembered the vow he had taken with his friends.

If I keep my word, how hungry I shall be by evening! he thought. I'd better make sure that there's plenty to eat once the fast is over. He set off towards the river.

A fisherman had caught several large fish early that morning, and had buried them in the sand, planning to return for them later. The otter soon smelt them out.

'A supper all ready for me!' he said to himself. 'But since it's a holy day, I mustn't steal.' Instead he called out: 'Does anyone own this fish?'

There being no answer, the otter carried the fish off to his home, setting it aside for his evening meal. Then he locked his front door and slept all through the day, undisturbed by beggars or holy men asking for alms.

Both the monkey and the jackal felt much the same way when they got up that morning. They remembered their vows but thought it best to have something put by for the evening. The jackal found some stale meat in someone's back yard. Ah, that should improve with age, he thought, and took it home for his evening meal. And the monkey climbed a mango tree and picked a bunch of mangoes. Like the otter, they decided to sleep through the day.

The hare woke early. Shaking his long ears, he came out of his burrow and sniffed the dew-drenched grass.

When evening comes, I can have my fill of grass, he thought. But if a beggar or holy man comes my way, what can I give him? I cannot offer him grass, and I have nothing else to give. I shall have to offer myself. Most men seem to relish the flesh of the hare. We're good to eat, I'm told. And pleased with this solution to the problem, he scampered off.

Now the God Sakka had been resting on a cloud not far away, and he had heard the hare speaking aloud.

'I will test him,' said the god. 'Surely no hare can be so noble and unselfish.'

Towards evening, God Sakka descended from his cloud, and assuming the form of an old priest, he sat down near the hare's burrow. When the animal came home from his romp, he said:

'Good evening, little hare. Can you give me something to eat? I have been fasting all day, and am so hungry that I cannot pray.'

The hare, remembering his vow, said: 'Is it true that men enjoy eating the flesh of the hare?'

'Quite true,' said the priest.

'In that case,' said the hare, 'since I have no other food to offer you, you can make a meal of me.'

'But I am a holy man, and this is a holy day, and I may not kill any living creature with my own hands.'

'Then collect some dry sticks and set them alight. I will leap into the flames myself, and when I am roasted you can eat me.'

God Sakka marvelled at these words, but he was still not quite convinced, so he caused a fire to spring up from the earth. The hare, without any hesitation, jumped into the flames.

'What's happening?' called the hare after a while. 'The fire surrounds me, but not a hair of my coat is singed. In fact, I'm feeling quite cold!'

As the hare spoke, the fire died down, and he found himself sitting on the cool sweet grass. Instead of the old priest, there stood before him the God Sakka in all his radiance.

'I am God Sakka, little hare, and having heard your vow, I wanted to test your sincerity. Such unselfishness of yours deserves immortality. It must be known throughout the world.'

God Sakka then stretched out his hand towards the mountain, and drew from it some of the essence which ran in its veins. This he threw towards the moon, which had just risen, and instantly the outline of the hare appeared on the moon's surface.

Then leaving the hare in a bed of sweet grass, he said: 'For ever and ever, little hare, you shall look down from the moon upon the world, to remind men of the old truth, "Give to others, and the gods will give to you."'

THE OWL

At night, when all is still,
The forest's sentinel
Glides silently across the hill
And perches in an old pine tree.
A friendly presence his!
No harm can come
From a night bird on the prowl.
His cry is mellow,
Much softer than a peacock's call.
Why then this fear of owls
Calling in the night?
If men must speak,
Then owls must hoot—
They have the right.
On me it casts no spell:
Rather, it seems to cry,
'The night is good—all's well, all's well.'

THE SNAKE

When, after days of rain,
The sun appears,
The snake emerges,
Green-gold on the grass.
Kept in so long,
He basks for hours,
Soaks up the hot bright sun.
Knowing how shy he is of me,
I walk a gentle pace,
Letting him doze in peace.
But to the snake, earth-bound,
Each step must sound like thunder.
He glides away,
Goes underground.
I've known him for some years:
A harmless green grass-snake,
Who, when he sees me on the path,
Uncoils and disappears.

CROSSING THE ROAD

Samuel was a snail of some individuality. Some considered him to be the bad snail in the family, but that was because he did not listen to his elders but liked to do things in his own way, trying out new plants or venturing into forbidden places. Birds and butterflies recognized no man-made borders, so why should snails? They'd been around longer than humans and were likely to be around even longer.

Not that Samuel had any global ambitions. It was just that the cabbage patch in which he and his fellow snails had been living did not appeal to him any more. He was heartily sick of cabbage leaves. And just across a busy road—his international boundary—was a field full of delicious-looking lettuce. And any snail would prefer lettuce to cabbage.

The trouble was, it was a very busy road, linking one city to another, and on it flowed a constant stream of cars, trucks, motorcycles, bicycles, vans, even the occasional steamroller. Samuel did not like the idea of being crushed under a steamroller. There were better ways of exiting planet earth—being swallowed by a large stork, for instance.

And then, of course, snails can't run. With the help of a little of their own juices, they glide slowly and leisurely over grass and weed and pebbles, in search of a juicy leaf or the company of a fellow snail. They were not made to run. They are not predators like the larger carnivores. Nor do they prey on each other like humans. They are all for minding their own business. And now here was Samuel, making it his business to invade that lettuce patch on the other side of the road.

Well, nothing ventured nothing gained. And ignoring the warnings of friends and familiars, Samuel set out to cross that life-threatening road. He could, of course, have waited until it was dark, but the road would have been no safer then. A constant stream of container trucks came thundering down the highway all through the night.

Tentacles waving, he began his stately crawl across the road.

Almost immediately he was nearly run over by a boy on a bicycle. Instinctively, Samuel withdrew into his little shell. Not that it would have made any difference. It might have protected him from a small bird, but not from a cycle tyre.

Samuel looked up and down the road. It was a single-width road, and vehicles could approach from either direction. It appeared to be clear at the moment.

Samuel advanced, covering a distance of some twelve inches in sixty seconds flat.

Then—*woosh*—a car sped by, its tyres missing Samuel by inches. He was almost blown away by a cloud of dust and exhaust fumes.

And then came another car. Samuel cringed. And survived. And wondered if he should turn around and go back the way he came. But snails aren't great thinkers. The lettuce patch was all that mattered.

Samuel had advanced by two or three feet when there came a deep, rumbling sound and he felt the ground quiver beneath him. A huge truck was bearing down on him!

Sometimes it is an advantage to be small. Samuel was somewhere in the middle of the road, and nowhere near the wheels when the truck thundered over him. All the same he was dazed and shaken, unable to move any further. Soon another truck would be coming along. Or was it a tractor that was chugging along towards him?

Just then there was a squeal of brakes, a blare of horns, and a tremendous crash. The truck had hit an oncoming car and both had veered off the road and were lying in a ditch. For a time all traffic ceased. Samuel emitted a slimy jet and began to crawl again. Then there was a burst of activity.

A motorcycle came tearing down the road, whizzing past a bewildered Samuel, and then stopping at the accident site. A policeman dismounted. In the distance a siren wailed. An ambulance was on its way.

And then it began to rain, a gentle patter on the tarmac. Refreshed, Samuel slid forward. The rain came down harder, and a fallen peepul leaf came sailing towards Samuel. It stopped beside him and Samuel crawled to the leaf. A spurt of rainwater picked up the leaf and sent it sailing across the remainder of the road and onto the grass verge.

Excelsior!

Samuel was home if not dry.

The lettuce field stretched before him. Motor horns and ambulance sirens melted into the distance. Humans could take care of themselves. So could snails! It would take him weeks to munch his way through a small corner of that lettuce patch, but he was going to try. To the winner the spoils!

The rain stopped and he began his feast.

The lettuce was all right, but it wasn't much better than the cabbage field he had left a little over an hour ago. Had the journey been worthwhile? Could he cross that road again? The odds were against survival.

He'd just have to settle down in this new and unfamiliar world. The grass is always greener on the other side—until you get there!

A SPECIAL TREE

One day, when Rakesh was six, he walked home from the Mussoorie bazaar eating cherries. They were a little sweet, a little sour; small, bright red cherries, which had come all the way from the Kashmir Valley.

Here in the Himalayan foothills where Rakesh lived, there were not many fruit trees. The soil was stony, and the dry cold winds stunted the growth of most plants. But on the more sheltered slopes there were forests of oak and deodar.

Rakesh lived with his grandfather on the outskirts of Mussoorie, just where the forest began. His father and mother lived in a small village fifty miles away, where they grew maize and rice and barley in narrow terraced fields on the lower slopes of the mountain. But there were no schools in the village, and Rakesh's parents were keen that he should go to school. As soon as he was of school-going age, they sent him to stay with his grandfather in Mussoorie. He had a little cottage outside the town.

Rakesh was on his way home from school when he bought the cherries. He paid fifty paise for the bunch. It took him about half an hour to walk home, and by the time he reached the cottage there were only three cherries left.

'Have a cherry, Grandfather,' he said, as soon as he saw his grandfather in the garden.

Grandfather took one cherry and Rakesh promptly ate the

other two. He kept the last seed in his mouth for some time, rolling it round and round on his tongue until all the tang had gone. Then he placed the seed on the palm of his hand and studied it.

'Are cherry seeds lucky?' asked Rakesh.

'Of course.'

'Then I'll keep it.'

'Nothing is lucky if you put it away. If you want luck, you must put it to some use.'

'What can I do with a seed?'

'Plant it.'

So Rakesh found a small space and began to dig up a flowerbed.

'Hey, not there,' said Grandfather, 'I've sown mustard in that bed. Plant it in that shady corner, where it won't be disturbed.'

Rakesh went to a corner of the garden where the earth was soft and yielding. He did not have to dig. He pressed the seed into the soil with his thumb and it went right in.

Then he had his lunch, and ran off to play cricket with his friends, and forgot all about the cherry seed.

When it was winter in the hills, a cold wind blew down from the snows and went *whoo-whoo-whoo* in the deodar trees, and the garden was dry and bare. In the evenings, Grandfather and Rakesh sat over a charcoal fire, and Grandfather told Rakesh stories—stories about people who turned into animals, and ghosts who lived in trees, and beans that jumped and stones that wept—and in turn Rakesh would read to him from the newspaper, Grandfather's eyesight being rather weak. Rakesh found the newspaper very dull—especially after the stories—but Grandfather wanted all the news...

They knew it was spring when the wild duck flew north

again, to Siberia. Early in the morning, when he got up to chop wood and light a fire, Rakesh saw the V-shaped formation streaming northward, the calls of the birds carrying clearly through the thin mountain air.

One morning in the garden he bent to pick up what he thought was a small twig and found to his surprise that it was well rooted. He stared at it for a moment, then ran to fetch Grandfather, calling, 'Dada, come and look, the cherry tree has come up!'

'What cherry tree?' asked Grandfather, who had forgotten about it.

'The seed we planted last year—look, it's come up!'

Rakesh went down on his haunches, while Grandfather bent almost double and peered down at the tiny tree. It was about four inches high.

'Yes, it's a cherry tree,' said Grandfather. 'You should water it now and then.'

Rakesh ran indoors and came back with a bucket of water.

'Don't drown it!' said Grandfather.

Rakesh gave it a sprinkling and circled it with pebbles.

'What are the pebbles for?' asked Grandfather.

'For privacy,' said Rakesh.

He looked at the tree every morning but it did not seem to be growing very fast, so he stopped looking at it except quickly, out of the corner of his eye. And, after a week or two, when he allowed himself to look at it properly, he found that it had grown—at least an inch!

That year the monsoon rains came early and Rakesh plodded to and from school in raincoat and chappals. Ferns sprang from the trunks of trees, strange-looking lilies came up in the long grass, and even when it wasn't raining the trees dripped and mist came curling up the valley. The cherry tree grew quickly in this season.

It was about two feet high when a goat entered the garden and ate all the leaves. Only the main stem and two thin branches remained.

'Never mind,' said Grandfather, seeing that Rakesh was upset. 'It will grow again, cherry trees are tough.'

Towards the end of the rainy season new leaves appeared on the tree. Then a woman cutting grass scrambled down the hillside, her scythe swishing through the heavy monsoon foliage. She did not try to avoid the tree: one sweep, and the cherry tree was cut in two.

When Grandfather saw what had happened, he went after the woman and scolded her; but the damage could not be repaired.

'Maybe it will die now,' said Rakesh.

'Maybe,' said Grandfather.

But the cherry tree had no intention of dying.

By the time summer came round again, it had sent out several new shoots with tender green leaves. Rakesh had grown taller too. He was eight now, a sturdy boy with curly black hair and deep black eyes. 'Blackberry eyes,' Grandfather called them.

That monsoon Rakesh went home to his village, to help his father and mother with the planting and ploughing and sowing. He was thinner but stronger when he came back to Grandfather's house at the end of the rains to find that the cherry tree had grown another foot. It was now up to his chest.

Even when there was rain, Rakesh would sometimes water the tree. He wanted it to know that he was there.

One day he found a bright green praying-mantis perched on a branch, peering at him with bulging eyes. Rakesh let it remain there; it was the cherry tree's first visitor.

The next visitor was a hairy caterpillar, who started making a meal of the leaves. Rakesh removed it quickly and dropped it on a heap of dry leaves.

'Come back when you're a butterfly,' he said.

Winter came early. The cherry tree bent low with the weight of snow. Field mice sought shelter in the roof of the cottage. The road from the valley was blocked, and for several days there was no newspaper, and this made Grandfather quite grumpy. His stories began to have unhappy endings.

In February, it was Rakesh's birthday. He was nine—and the tree was four, but almost as tall as Rakesh.

One morning, when the sun came out, Grandfather came into the garden to 'let some warmth get into my bones,' as he put it. He stopped in front of the cherry tree, stared at it for a few moments, and then called out, 'Rakesh! Come and look! Come quickly before it falls!'

Rakesh and Grandfather gazed at the tree as though it had performed a miracle. There was a pale pink blossom at the end of a branch.

The following year there were more blossoms. And suddenly the tree was taller than Rakesh, even though it was less than half his age. And then it was taller than Grandfather, who was older than some of the oak trees.

But Rakesh had grown too. He could run and jump and climb trees as well as most boys, and he read a lot of books, although he still liked listening to Grandfather's tales.

In the cherry tree, bees came to feed on the nectar in the blossoms, and tiny birds pecked at the blossoms and broke them off. But the tree kept blossoming right through the spring, and there were always more blossoms than birds.

That summer there were small cherries on the tree. Rakesh tasted one and spat it out.

'It's too sour,' he said.

'They'll be better next year,' said Grandfather.

But the birds liked them—especially the bigger birds, such as the bulbuls and scarlet minivets—and they flitted in and out of the foliage, feasting on the cherries.

On a warm sunny afternoon, when even the bees looked sleepy, Rakesh was looking for Grandfather without finding him in any of his favourite places around the house. Then he looked out of the bedroom window and saw Grandfather reclining on a cane chair under the cherry tree.

'There's just the right amount of shade here,' said Grandfather. 'And I like looking at the leaves.'

'They're pretty leaves,' said Rakesh. 'And they are always ready to dance if there's a breeze.'

After Grandfather had come indoors, Rakesh went into the garden and lay down on the grass beneath the tree. He gazed up through the leaves at the great blue sky; and turning on his side, he could see the mountains striding away into the clouds. He was still lying beneath the tree when the evening shadows crept across the garden. Grandfather came back and sat down beside Rakesh, and they waited in silence until the stars came out and the nightjar began to call. In the forest below, the crickets and cicadas began tuning up; and suddenly the trees were full of the sound of insects.

'There are so many trees in the forest,' said Rakesh. 'What's so special about this tree? Why do we like it so much?'

'We planted it ourselves,' said Grandfather. 'That's why it's special.'

'Just one small seed,' said Rakesh, and he touched the

smooth bark of the tree that he had grown. He ran his hand along the trunk of the tree and put his finger to the tip of a leaf. 'I wonder,' he whispered. 'Is this what it feels to be God?'

THOSE SIMPLE THINGS

It's the *simple* things in life that keep us from going crazy. Like that pigeon in the skylight in the New Delhi Nursing Home where I was incarcerated for two or three days. Even worse than the illness that had brought me there were the series of tests that the doctors insisted I had to go through—gastroscopies, endoscopies, X-rays, blood tests, urine tests, probes into any orifice they could find, and at the end of it all a nice fat bill designed to give me a heart attack.

The only thing that prevented me from running into the street, shouting for help, was that pigeon in the skylight. It sheltered there at various times during the day, and its gentle cooing soothed my nerves and kept me in touch with the normal world outside. I owe my sanity to that pigeon.

Which reminds me of the mouse who shared my little bed-sitting room in London, when I was just seventeen and all on my own. Those early months in London were lonely times for a shy young man going to work during the day and coming back to a cold, damp, empty room late in the evening. In the morning, I would make myself a hurried breakfast, and at night I'd make myself a cheese or ham sandwich. This was when I noticed the little mouse peeping out at me from behind the books I had piled up on the floor, there being no bookshelf. I threw some crumbs in his direction, and he was soon making a meal of them and a piece of cheese. After that, he would present himself before me every evening, and the room was no longer as empty and lonely as when I had first moved in.

He was a smart little mouse and sometimes he would speak to me—sharp little squeaks to remind me it was dinner time.

Months later, when I moved to another part of London, I had to leave him behind—I did not want to deprive him of friends and family—but it was a fat little mouse I left behind.

During my three years in London I must have lived in at least half a dozen different lodging houses, and the rooms were usually dull and depressing. One had a window looking out on a railway track; another provided me with a great view of a cemetery. To spend my day off looking down upon hundreds of graves was hardly uplifting, even if some of the tombstones were beautifully sculpted. No wonder I spent my evenings watching old Marx Brothers films at the Everyman Cinema nearby.

Living in small rooms for the greater part of my life, I have always felt the need for small, familiar objects that become a part of me, even if sometimes I forget to say hello to them. A glass paperweight, a laughing Buddha, an old horseshoe, a print of Hokusai's *Great Wave*, a suitcase that has seen better days, an old school tie (never worn, but there all the same), a gramophone record (can't play it now, but when I look at it, the song comes back to me), a potted fern, an old address book… Where have they gone, those old familiar faces? Not one address is relevant today (after some forty years), but I keep it all the same.

I turn to a page at the end, and discover why I have kept it all these years. It holds a secret, scribbled note to an early love:

> 'I did not sleep last night, for you had kissed me. You held my hand and put it to your cheek and to your breasts.

> And I had closed your eyes and kissed them, and taken your face in my hands and touched your lips with mine. And then, my darling, I stumbled into the light like a man intoxicated, and did not know what people were saying or doing...'

Gosh! How romantic I was at thirty! And reading that little entry, I feel like going out and falling in love again. But will anyone fall in love with an old man of seventy-five?

Yes! There's a little mouse in my room.

THOSE THREE BEARS

Most Himalayan villages lie in the valleys where there are small streams, some farmland, and protection from the biting winds that come through the mountain passes in winter. The houses are usually made of large stones and have sloping slate roofs so the heavy monsoon rain can run off easily. During the sunny autumn months, the roofs are often covered with pumpkins, left there to ripen in the sun.

One October night, when I was sleeping at a friend's house in a village in these hills, I was awakened by a rumbling and thumping on the roof. I woke my friend and asked him what was happening.

'It's only a bear,' he said.

'Is it trying to get in?'

'No. It's after the pumpkins.'

A little later, when we looked out a window, we saw a black bear making off through a field, leaving a trail of half-eaten pumpkins.

Face to Face

In winter, when snow covers the higher ranges, the Himalayan bears come to lower altitudes in search of food. Sometimes they forage in fields and, because they are short-sighted and suspicious of anything that moves, they can be dangerous. But, like most wild animals, they avoid humans as much as possible.

Village folk always advise me to run downhill if chased by a bear. They say bears find it easier to run uphill than down. I am yet to be chased by a bear, and will happily skip the experience. But I have seen a few of these mountain bears in India, and they are always fascinating to watch.

Himalayan bears enjoy pumpkins, corn, plums, and apricots. Once, while I was sitting in an oak tree hoping to see a pair of pine martens that lived nearby, I heard the whining grumble of a bear, and presently, a small bear ambled into the clearing beneath the tree.

He was little more than a cub, and I was not alarmed. I sat very still, waiting to see what he would do.

He put his nose to the ground and sniffed his way along until he came to a large anthill. Here he began huffing and puffing, blowing rapidly in and out of his nostrils, so that the dust from the anthill flew in all directions. But the anthill had been deserted, and so, grumbling, the bear made his way up a nearby plum tree. Soon he was perched high in the branches. It was then that he saw me.

The bear at once scrambled several feet higher up the tree and lay flat on a branch. Since it wasn't a very big branch, there was a lot of bear showing on either side. He tucked his head behind another branch. He could no longer see me, so he apparently was satisfied that he was hidden, although he couldn't help grumbling.

Like all bears, this one was full of curiosity. So, slowly, inch by inch, his black snout appeared over the edge of the branch. As soon as he saw me, he drew his head back and hid his face.

He did this several times. I waited until he wasn't looking, then moved some way down my tree. When the bear looked over and saw that I was missing, he was so pleased that he stretched right across to another branch and helped himself to a plum. I couldn't help bursting into laughter.

The startled young bear tumbled out of the tree, dropped through the branches some fifteen feet, and landed with a thump in a pile of dried leaves. He was unhurt, but fled from the clearing, grunting and squealing all the way.

The Flag 'Bearer'

Another time, my friend Prem told me, a bear had been active in his cornfield. We took up a post at night in an old cattle shed, which gave a clear view of the moonlit field.

A little after midnight, a female bear came down to the edge of the field. She seemed to sense that we had been about. She was hungry, however. So, after standing on her hind legs and peering around to make sure the field was empty, she came cautiously out of the forest.

Her attention was soon distracted by some Tibetan prayer flags, which had been strung between two trees. She gave a grunt of disapproval and began to back away, but the fluttering of the flags was a puzzle that she wanted to solve. So she stopped and watched them.

Soon the bear advanced to within a few feet of the flags, examining them from various angles. Then, seeing that they posed no danger, she went right up to the flags and pulled them down. Grunting with apparent satisfaction, she moved into the field of corn.

Prem had decided that he didn't want to lose any more of his crop, so he started shouting. His children woke up and soon came running from the house, banging on empty kerosene tins.

Deprived of her dinner, the bear made off in a bad temper. She ran downhill at a good speed, and I was glad that I was not in her way.

Uphill or downhill, an angry bear is best given a very wide berth.

THE ELEPHANT AND THE CASSOWARY

The baby elephant wasn't out of place in our home in north India because India is where elephants belong, and in any case our house was full of pets brought home by Grandfather, who was in the Forest Service. But the cassowary bird was different. No one had ever seen such a bird before—not in India, at least. Grandfather had picked it up on a voyage to Singapore, where he'd been given the bird by a rubber planter who'd got it from a Dutch trader who'd got it, from a man in Indonesia.

Anyway, it ended up at our home in Dehra, and seemed to do quite well in the subtropical climate. It looked like a cross between a turkey and an ostrich, but bigger than the former, and smaller than the latter—about five feet in height. It was not a beautiful bird, nor even a friendly one, but it had come to stay, and everyone was curious about it especially the baby elephants.

Right from the start, the baby elephant took a great interest in the cassowary, a bird unlike any found in the Indian jungles.

He would circle round the odd creature and diffidently examine with his trunk the texture of its stumpy wings; of course, he suspected no evil, and his childlike curiosity encouraged him to take liberties which resulted in an unpleasant experience.

Noticing the baby elephant's attempts to make friends with

the rather morose cassowary, we felt a bit apprehensive. Self-contained and sullen, the big bird responded only by slowly and slyly raising one of its powerful legs, in the meantime gazing into space with an innocent air. We knew what the gesture meant; we had seen that treacherous leg raised on many an occasion, and suddenly shooting out with a force that would have done credit to a vicious camel. In fact, camel and cassowary kicks are delivered in the same way, except that the camel kicks backward like a horse and the bird forward.

We wished to spare our baby elephant a painful experience, and led him away from the bird. But he persisted in his friendly overtures, and one morning he received an ugly reward. Rapid as lightning, the cassowary hit straight from the hip and knee joints, and the elephant ran squealing to Grandmother.

For several days he avoided the cassowary, and we thought he had learnt his lesson. He crossed and recrossed the compound and the garden, swinging his trunk, thinking furiously. Then, about a week later, he appeared on the veranda at breakfast time in his usual cheery, childlike fashion, sidling up to the cassowary as if nothing had happened.

We were struck with amazement at this and so, it seemed, was the bird. Had the painful lesson already been forgotten, and by a member of the elephant tribe noted for its ability never to forget? Another dose of the same medicine would serve the baby right.

The cassowary once more began to draw up its fighting leg with sinister determination. It was nearing the true position for the master kick, kung-fu style, when all of a sudden the baby elephant seized with his trunk the cassowary's other leg and pulled it down. There was a clumsy flapping of wings, a tremendous swelling of the bird's wattle, and an undignified getting up, as if it were a floored boxer doing his best to beat the count of ten. The bird then marched off with an attempt to look stately and unconcerned, while we at the breakfast table were convulsed with laughter.

After this the cassowary bird gave the baby elephant as wide a berth as possible. But they were not forced to coexist for very long. The baby elephant, getting bulky and cumbersome, was sold and now lives in a zoological garden where he is a favourite with young visitors who love to take rides on his back.

As for the cassowary, he continued to grace our veranda for many years, gaped at, but not made much of, while entering a rather friendless old age.

HENRY: A CHAMELEON

This is the story of Henry, our pet chameleon. Chameleons are in a class by themselves and are no ordinary reptiles. They are easily distinguished from their nearest relatives, the lizards, by certain outstanding features. A chameleon's tongue is as long as its body. Its limbs are long and slender and its fingers and toes resemble a parrot's claws. On its head may be any of several ornaments. Henry had a rigid crest that looked like a fireman's helmet.

Henry's eyes were his most remarkable feature. They were not beautiful, but his left eye was quite independent of his right. He could move one eye without disturbing the other. Each eyeball, bulging out of his head, wobbled up and down, backward and forward. This frenzied movement gave Henry a horrible squint. And one look into Henry's frightful gaze was often enough to scare people into believing that chameleons are dangerous and poisonous reptiles.

One day, Grandfather was visiting a friend, when he came upon a noisy scene at the garden gate. Men were shouting, hurling stones, and brandishing sticks. The cause of the uproar was a chameleon that had been discovered sunning itself on a shrub. Someone claimed that the chameleon could poison people twenty feet away, simply by spitting at them. The residents of the area had risen up in arms. Grandfather was just in time to save the chameleon from certain death—he brought the little reptile home.

That chameleon was Henry, and that was how he came to live with us.

When I first visited Henry, he would treat me with great caution, sitting perfectly still on his perch with his back to me. The eye nearer to me would move around like the beam of a searchlight until it had me well in focus. Then it would stop and the other eye would begin an independent survey of its own. For a long time Henry trusted no one and responded to my friendliest gestures with grave suspicion.

Tiring of his wary attitude, I would tickle him gently in the ribs with my finger. This always threw him into a great rage. He would blow himself up to an enormous size as his lungs filled up with air, while his colour changed from green to red. He would sit up on his hind legs, swaying from side to side, hoping to overawe me. Opening his mouth very wide, he would let out an angry hiss. But his threatening display went no further. He did not bite.

Henry was a harmless fellow. If I put my finger in his mouth, even during his wildest moments, he would simply wait for me to take it out again. I suppose he could bite. His rigid jaws carried a number of finely pointed teeth. But Henry seemed convinced that his teeth were there for the sole purpose of chewing food, not fingers.

Henry was sometimes willing to take food from my hands. This he did very swiftly. His tongue performed like a boomerang and always came back to him with the food, usually an insect, attached to it.

Although Henry didn't cause any trouble in our house, he did create somewhat of a riot in the nursery down the road. It started out quite innocently.

When the papayas in our orchard were ripe, Grandmother

sent a basketful to her friend Mrs Ghosh, who was the principal of the nursery school. While the basket sat waiting, Henry went searching for beetles and slipped in among the papayas, unnoticed. The gardener dutifully carried the basket to the school and left it in Mrs Ghosh's office. When Mrs Ghosh returned after making her rounds, she began examining and admiring the papayas. And out popped Henry.

Mrs Ghosh screamed. Henry squinted up at her, both eyes revolving furiously. Mrs Ghosh screamed again. Henry's colour changed from green to yellow to red. His mouth opened as though he, too, would like to scream. An assistant teacher rushed in, took one look at the chameleon, and joined in the shrieking.

Henry was terrified. He fled from the office, running down the corridor and into one of the classrooms. There he climbed up on a desk while children ran in all directions—some to get away from Henry, some to catch him. Henry finally made his exit through a window and disappeared in the garden.

Grandmother heard about the incident from Mrs Ghosh but didn't mention that the chameleon was ours. It might have spoiled their friendship.

Grandfather and I didn't think Henry would find his way back to us, because the school was three blocks away. But a few days later, I found him sunning himself on the garden wall. Although he looked none the worse for his adventure, he never went abroad again. Henry spent the rest of his days in the garden, where he kept the insect population well within bounds.

OWLS IN THE FAMILY

One morning we found a full-fledged baby spotted owlet on the ground by the verandah steps. When Grandfather picked it up, it hissed and clacked its bill, but, after a meal of raw meat and water, settled down for the day under my bed.

The spotted owlet, even when full grown, is only the size of a myna, and has none of the sinister appearance of the larger owls. A pair of them may often be found in an old mango or tamarind tree, and by tapping on the tree trunk you may be able to persuade the bird to show an enquiring face at the entrance to its hole. The bird is not normally afraid of man, nor is it strictly a night-bird; but it prefers to stay at home during the day, as it is sometimes attacked by other birds, who consider all owls as their enemies.

The little owlet was quite happy under my bed. The following day a second owlet was found in almost the same place on the verandah, and only then did we realize that where the rainwater pipe emerged through the roof, there was a rough sort of nest, from which the birds had fallen. We took the second young owl to join the first, and fed them both. When I went to bed, they were on the ledge just inside the mosquito netting, and later in the night their mother found them there. From outside she crooned and gurgled for a long time, and in the morning I found that she had left a mouse with its tail tucked through the mosquito net! Obviously, she placed no reliance on me as a foster-parent.

The young birds throve and, ten days later at dawn, Grandfather and I took them into the garden to release them. I had placed one on a branch of the mango tree, and was stooping to pick up the other, when I received quite a heavy blow on the back of my head. A second or two later, the mother owl swooped down at Grandfather, but he was agile enough to duck out of its way. Quickly, I placed the second owl under the mango tree. Then from it safe distance we watched the mother fly down and lead her offspring into the long grass at the edge of the garden.

We thought she would take her family away from the vicinity of our rather strange household; but next morning, on coming out of my room, I found two young owls standing on the wall just outside the door! I ran to tell Grandfather, and when we came back we found the mother sitting on the bird-bath ten yards away. She was evidently feeling sorry for her behaviour the previous day, because she greeted us with a soft 'whoo-whoo'.

'Now, there's an unselfish mother for you!' said Grandfather. 'It's obvious she'd like them to have a good home. And they're probably getting a bit too big for her to manage.'

So the two owlets became regular members of our household, and, strangely enough, were among the few pets that Grandmother took a liking to. She objected to all snakes, most monkeys, and some crows, but she took quite a fancy to the owls, and frequently fed them on spaghetti. They seemed quite fond of spaghetti. In fact, the owls became so attached to Grandmother that they began to show affection towards anyone in a petticoat, including Aunt Mabel, who was terrified of them. She would run shrieking from the room every time one of the birds sidled up to her in a friendly manner.

Forgetful of the fact that Grandfather and I had reared

them, the owls would sometimes swell their feathers and snap at anyone in trousers. To avoid displeasing them, Grandfather wore a petticoat at feeding time. This mild form of transvestism appeared to satisfy them. I compromised by wearing an apron.

In response to Grandmother's voice, the owlets would make sounds as gentle and soothing as the purring of a cat; but when wild owls were around, ours would rend the night with blood-curdling shrieks. Their nightly occupation was catching beetles, with which the kitchen-quarters were infested at the time. With their sharp eyes and powerful beaks they were excellent pest destroyers.

The owls loved to sit and splash in a shallow dish, especially if cold water was poured over them from a jug at the same time. They would get thoroughly wet, jump out on to a perch, shake themselves, then return for a second splash and sometimes a third. During the day they dozed in large cages under the trees in the garden. They needed cages for protection against attacks from wild birds. At night they had the freedom of the house, where they exercised their wings as much as they liked. Superstitious folk, who dread the cry of the owl, may be interested to know that—mice excepted—there were no untoward deaths in the house during the owls' residence.

Looking back on those owlish days, I carry in my mind a picture of Grandmother with a contented look in her rocking chair. Once, on entering her room while she was having an afternoon nap, I saw that one of the owls had crawled up her pillow till its head was snuggled under her ear. Both Grandmother and the little owl were snoring.

RANJI'S WONDERFUL BAT

'How's that!' shouted the wicketkeeper, holding the ball up in his gloves.

'How's that!' echoed the slip fielders.

'How?' growled the fast bowler; glaring at the umpire.

'Out!' said the umpire.

And Suraj, the captain of the school team, was walking slowly back to the pavilion—which was really a tool shed at the end of the field.

The score stood at 53 runs for 4 wickets. Another 60 runs had to be made for victory, and only one good batsman remained. All the rest were bowlers who couldn't be expected to make many runs.

It was Ranji's turn to bat.

He was the youngest member of the team, only eleven, but sturdy and full of pluck. As he walked briskly to the wicket, his unruly black hair was blown about by a cool breeze that came down from the hills.

Ranji had a good eye and strong wrists, and had made lots of runs in some of the minor matches. But in the last two inter-school games, his scores had been poor, the highest being 12 runs. Today he was determined to make enough runs to take his side to victory.

Ranji took his guard and prepared to face the bowler. The fielders moved closer, in anticipation of another catch. The tall fast bowler scowled and began his long run. His arm whirled over, and the hard, shiny red ball came hurtling towards Ranji.

Ranji was going to lunge forward and play the ball back to the bowler, but at the last moment he changed his mind and stepped back, intending to push the ball through the ring of fielders on his right or offside.

'How's that!' screamed the bowler hopping about like a kangaroo.

'How?' shouted the wicketkeeper.

The umpire slowly raised a finger.

'Out,' he said.

'Never mind,' said Suraj, patting Ranji on the back. 'You'll do better next time. You're out of form just now, that's all.'

'You'll have to make more runs in the next game,' he told Ranji, 'or you'll lose your place in the side!'

Avoiding the other players, Ranji slowly walked homewards, his head down, his hands in his pockets. He was very upset. He had been trying so hard and practising so regularly, but when an important game came along he failed to make a big score. It seemed that there was nothing he could do about it. But he loved playing cricket, and he couldn't bear the thought of being out of the school team.

On his way home he had to pass the clock tower, where he often stopped at Mr Kumar's Sports Shop, to chat with the owner or look at all the things on the shelves: footballs, cricket balls, badminton rackets, hockey sticks, balls of various shapes and sizes—it was a wonderland where Ranji liked to linger every day.

But this was one day when he didn't feel like stopping. He looked the other way and was about to cross the road when Mr Kumar's voice stopped him.

'Hello, Ranji! Off in a hurry today? And why are you looking so sad?'

So Ranji had to stop and say namaste. He couldn't ignore Mr Kumar, who had always been so kind and helpful, often giving him advice on how to bowl in different styles. Mr Kumar had been a state-level player once, and had scored a century in a match against Tanzania. Now he liked encouraging young players and he thought Ranji would make a good cricketer.

'What's the trouble?' he asked as Ranji stepped into the shop. Because Mr Kumar was so friendly, the sports merchandise also seemed friendly. The bats and balls and shuttlecocks all seemed to want to be helpful.

'We lost the match,' said Ranji.

'Never mind,' said Mr Kumar. 'Where would we be without losers? There wouldn't be any games without them—no cricket or football or hockey or tennis! No carom or marbles. No sports shop for me! Anyway, how many runs did you make?'

'None, I made a big round egg.'

Mr Kumar rested his hand on Ranji's shoulder. 'Never mind. All good players have a bad day now and then.'

'But I haven't made a good score in my last three matches,' said Ranji. 'I'll be dropped from the team if I don't do something in the next game.'

'Well, we can't have that happening,' mused Mr Kumar. 'Something will have to be done about it.'

'I'm just unlucky,' said Ranji.

'Maybe, maybe... But in that case, it's time your luck changed.'

'It's too late now,' said Ranji.

'Nonsense. It's never too late. Now, you just come with me to the back of the shop and I'll see if I can do something about your luck.'

Puzzled, Ranji followed Mr Kumar through the curtained partition at the back of the shop. He found himself in a badly-lit room stacked to the ceiling with all kinds of old and second-hand sporting goods—torn football bladders, broken bats, rackets without strings, broken darts and tattered badminton nets. Mr Kumar began examining a number of old cricket bats, and after a few minutes he said, 'Ah!' Picking up one of the bats he held it out to Ranji.

'This is it!' he said. 'This is the luckiest of all my old bats. This is the bat I made a century with!' He gave it a twirl and started hitting an imaginary ball to all corners of the room.

'Of course it's an old bat, but it hasn't lost any of its magic,' said Mr Kumar, pausing in his stroke-making to recover his breath. He held it out to Ranji. 'Here, take it!' I'll lend it to you for the rest of the cricket season. You won't fail with this with you.'

Ranji took the bat and looked at it with awe and delight.

'Is it really the bat you made a century with?' he asked.

'It is,' said Mr Kumar. 'And it may get you a hundred runs too!'

Ranji spent a nervous week waiting for Saturday's match. His school team would be playing against a strong side from another town. There was a lot of classwork that week, so Ranji did not get much time to practise with the other boys. As he had no brothers or sisters he asked Koki, the girl next door, to bowl to him in the garden. Koki bowled quite well, but Ranji liked to hit the ball hard—'just to get used to the bat,' he told her—and she soon got tired of chasing the ball all over the garden.

At last Saturday arrived, bright and sunny and just right for cricket.

Suraj won the toss for the school and chose batting first.

The opening batsmen put on 30 runs without being separated. The visiting fast bowlers couldn't do much. Then the spin bowlers came on, and immediately there was a change in the game. Two wickets fell in one over, and the score was 33 for 2. Suraj made a few quick runs, then he too was out to one of the spinners, caught behind the wicket. The next batsman was clean bowled—46 for 4—and it was Ranji's turn to bat.

He walked slowly to the wicket. The fielders crowded round him. He took guard and prepared for the first ball.

The bowler took a short run and then the ball was twirling towards Ranji, looking as though it would spin away from his bat as he leaned forward into his stroke.

And then a thrill ran through Ranji's arm as he felt the ball meet the springy willow of the bat.

Crack!

The ball, hit firmly with the middle of Ranji's bat, streaked past the helpless bowler and sped towards the boundary. Four runs!

The bowler was annoyed, with the result that his next ball was a loose full toss. Ranji swung it to the onside boundary for another four.

And that was only the beginning. Now, Ranji began to play all the strokes he knew: late cuts and square cuts, straight drives, on drives and off drives. The rival captain tried all his bowlers, fast and spin, but none of them could remove Ranji. Instead, he sent the fielders scampering to all corners of the field.

By the lunch break he had scored 40 runs. And twenty minutes after lunch, when Suraj closed the innings, Ranji was not out with 58.

The rival team was bowled out for a poor score, and Ranji's school won the match.

On his way home, Ranji stopped at Mr Kumar's shop to give him the good news.

'We won!' he said. 'And I made 58—my highest score so far. It really is a lucky bat!'

'I told you so,' said Mr Kumar, giving Ranji a warm handshake. 'There will be bigger scores yet.'

Ranji went home in high spirits. He was so pleased that he stopped at the Jumma Sweet Shop and bought two laddus for Koki. She was crazy about laddus.

Mr Kumar was right. It was only the beginning of Ranji's success with the bat. In the next game he scored 40, and was out when he grew careless and allowed himself to be stumped by the wicketkeeper. The game that followed was a two-day match, and Ranji, who was now batting at Number 3, made 45 runs. He hit a number of boundaries before being caught. In the second innings, when the school team needed only six runs for victory, Ranji was batting at 25 when the winning runs were hit.

Everyone was pleased with him—his coach, his captain, Suraj and Mr Kumar—but only one knew about the lucky bat. That was a secret between Ranji and Mr Kumar.

One evening, during an informal game on the maidan, Ranji's friend Bhim slipped while running after the ball, and cut his hand on a sharp stone. Ranji took him to a doctor near the clock tower, where the wound was washed and bandaged. As it was getting late, he decided to go straight home. Usually he walked, but that evening he caught a bus near the clock tower.

When he got home, his mother brought him a cup of tea, and while he was drinking it, Koki walked in, and the first thing she said was, 'Ranji, where's your bat?'

'Oh, I must have left it on the maidan when Bhim got hurt,' said Ranji, starting up and spilling his tea. 'I'd better go and get it now, or it will disappear.'

'You can fetch it tomorrow,' said his mother. 'It's getting dark.'

'I'll take a torch,' said Ranji.

He was worried about the bat.

Without it, his luck might desert him.

He hadn't the patience to wait for a bus, and ran all the way to the maidan.

The maidan was deserted, and there was no sign of the bat. And then Ranji remembered that he'd had it with him on the bus, after saying goodbye to Bhim at the clock tower. He must have left it on the bus!

Well, he'd never find it now. The bat was lost forever. And on Saturday Ranji's school would be playing their last and most important match of the cricket season against a public school team from Delhi.

Next day he was at Mr Kumar's shop, looking very sorry for himself.

'What's the matter?' asked Mr Kumar.

'I've lost the bat,' said Ranji. 'Your lucky bat. The one I made all my runs with! I left it in the bus. And the day after tomorrow we are playing the Delhi school, and I'll be out for a duck, and we'll lose our chance of being the champion school.'

Mr Kumar looked a little anxious at first; then he smiled and said, 'You can still make all the runs you want.'

'But I don't have the bat anymore,' said Ranji.

'Any bat will do,' said Mr Kumar.

'What do you mean?'

'I mean it's the batsman and not the bat that matters. Shall I tell you something? That old bat I gave you was no different from any other bat I've used. True, I made a lot of runs with it, but I made runs with other bats too. A bat has magic only when the batsman has magic! What you needed was confidence, not a bat. And by believing in the bat, you got your confidence back!'

'What's confidence?' asked Ranji. It was a new word for him.

'Confidence,' said Mr Kumar slowly, 'confidence is knowing you are good.'

'And I can be good without the bat?'

'Of course. You have always been good. You are good now. You will be good the day after tomorrow. Remember that. If you remember it, you'll make the runs.'

On Saturday, Ranji walked to the wicket with a bat borrowed from Bhim.

The school team had lost its first wicket with only two runs on the board. Ranji went in at this stage. The Delhi school's opening bowler was sending down some really fast ones. Ranji faced up to him.

The first ball was very fast but it wasn't on a good length. Quick on his feet, Ranji stepped back and pulled it hard to the onside boundary. The ball soared over the heads of the fielders and landed with a crash in a crate full of cold drink bottles.

A six! Everyone stood up and cheered.

And it was only the beginning of Ranji's wonderful innings.

The match ended in a draw, but Ranji's 75 was the talk of the school.

On his way home he bought a dozen laddus. Six for Koki and six for Mr Kumar.

LOOK FOR THE COLOURS OF LIFE

Colours are everywhere,
Bright blue the sky,
Dark green the forest
And light the fresh grass;
Bright yellow the lights
From a train sweeping past,
The Flame trees glow
At this time of year,
The mangoes burn bright
As the monsoon draws near.

A favourite colour of mine
Is the pink of the candy-floss man
As he comes down the dusty road,
Calling his wares;
And the balloon-man soon follows,
Selling his floating bright colours.

It's early summer
And the roses blush
In the dew-drenched dawn,
And poppies sway red and white
In the invisible breeze.
Only the wind has no colour:
But if you look carefully

You will see it teasing
The colour out of the leaves.
And the rain has no colour
But it turns the bronzed grass
To emerald green,
And gives a golden sheen
To the drenched sunflower.
Look for the colours of life—
They are everywhere,
Even in your dreams.

THE EYES OF THE EAGLE

It was a high, piercing sound, almost like the yelping of a dog. Jai stopped picking the wild strawberries that grew in the grass around him, and looked up at the sky. He had a dog—a shaggy guard dog called Motu—but Motu did not yet yelp, he growled and barked. The strange sound came from the sky, and Jai had heard it before. Now, realizing what it was, he jumped to his feet, calling to his dog, calling his sheep to start for home. Motu came bounding towards him, ready for a game.

'Not now, Motu!' said Jai. 'We must get the lambs home quickly.' Again he looked up at the sky.

He saw it now, a black speck against the sun, growing larger as it circled the mountain, coming lower every moment—a Golden Eagle, king of the skies over the higher Himalayas, ready now to swoop and seize its prey.

Had it seen a pheasant or a pine marten? Or was it after one of the lambs? Jai had never lost a lamb to an eagle, but recently some of the other shepherds had been talking about a golden eagle that had been preying on their flocks.

The sheep had wandered some way down the side of the mountain, and Jai ran after them to make sure that none of the lambs had gone off on its own.

Motu ran about, barking furiously. He wasn't very good at keeping the sheep together—he was often bumping into them and sending them tumbling down the slope—but his size and bear-like look kept the leopards and wolves at a distance.

Jai was counting the lambs; they were bleating loudly and staying close to their mothers. *One—two—three—four...*

There should have been a fifth. Jai couldn't see it on the slope below him. He looked up towards a rocky ledge near the steep path to the Tung temple. The golden eagle was circling the rocks.

The bird disappeared from sight for a moment, then rose again with a small creature grasped firmly in its terrible talons.

'It has taken a lamb!' shouted Jai. He started scrambling up the slope. Motu ran ahead of him, barking furiously at the big bird as it glided away over the tops of the stunted junipers to its eyrie on the cliffs above Tung.

There was nothing that Jai and Motu could do except stare helplessly and angrily at the disappearing eagle. The lamb had died the instant it had been struck. The rest of the flock seemed unaware of what had happened. They still grazed on the thick, sweet grass of the mountain slopes.

'We had better drive them home, Motu,' said Jai, and at a nod from the boy, the big dog bounded down the slope to take part in his favourite game of driving the sheep homewards. Soon he had them running all over the place, and Jai had to dash about trying to keep them together. Finally they straggled homewards.

'A fine lamb gone,' said Jai to himself gloomily. 'I wonder what Grandfather will say.'

Grandfather said, 'Never mind. It had to happen some day. That eagle has been watching the sheep for some time.'

Grandmother, more practical, said, 'We could have sold the lamb for three hundred rupees. You'll have to be more careful in future, Jai. Don't fall asleep on the hillside, and don't read storybooks when you are supposed to be watching the sheep!'

'I wasn't reading this morning,' said Jai truthfully, forgetting to mention that he had been gathering strawberries.

'It's good for him to read,' said Grandfather, who had never had the luck to go to school. In his days, there weren't any schools in the mountains. Now there was one in every village.

'Time enough to read at night,' said Grandmother, who did not think much of the little one-room school down at Maku, their home village.

'Well, these are the October holidays,' said Grandfather. 'Otherwise he would not be here to help us with the sheep. It will snow by the end of the month, and then we will move with the flock. You will have more time for reading then, Jai.'

At Maku, which was down in the warmer valley, Jai's parents tilled a few narrow terraces on which they grew barley, millets and potatoes. The old people brought their sheep up to the Tung meadows to graze during the summer months. They stayed in a small stone hut just off the path which pilgrims took to the ancient temple. At 12,000 feet above sea level, it was the highest Hindu temple on the inner Himalayan ranges.

The following day Jai and Motu were very careful. The did not let the sheep out of sight even for a minute. Nor did they catch sight of the golden eagle. 'What if it attacks again?' wondered Jai. 'How will I stop it?'

The great eagle, with its powerful beak and talons, was more than a match for boy or dog. Its hind claw, four inches round the curve, was its most dangerous weapon. When it spread its wings, the distance from tip to tip was more than eight feet.

The eagle did not come that day because it had fed well and was now resting in its eyrie. Old bones, which had belonged to pheasants, snow cocks, pine martens and even foxes, were scattered about the rocks which formed the eagle's home. The eagle had a mate, but it was not the breeding season and she was away on a scouting expedition of her own.

The golden eagle stood on its rocky ledge, staring majestically across the valley. Its hard, unblinking eyes missed nothing. Those strange orange-yellow eyes could spot a field rat or a mouse hare more than a hundred yards below.

There were other eagles on the mountain, but usually they kept to their own territory. And only the bolder ones went for lambs, because the flocks were always protected by men and dogs.

The eagle took off from its eyrie and glided gracefully, powerfully over the valley, circling the Tung mountain.

Below lay the old temple, built from slabs of grey granite. A line of pilgrims snaked up the steep, narrow path. On the meadows below the peak, the sheep grazed peacefully, unaware of the presence of the eagle. The great bird's shadow slid over the sunlit slopes.

The eagle saw the boy and the dog, but he did not fear them. He had his eye on a lamb that was frisking about on the grass, a few feet away from the other grazing sheep.

Jai did not see the eagle until it swept round an outcrop of rocks about a hundred feet away. It moved silently, without any movement of its wings, for it had already built up the momentum for its dive. Now it came straight at the lamb.

Motu saw the bird in time. With a low growl he dashed forward and reached the side of the lamb at almost the same instant that the eagle swept in.

There was a terrific collision. Feathers flew. The eagle screamed with rage. The lamb tumbled down the slope, and Motu howled in pain as the huge beak struck him high on the leg.

The big bird, a little stunned by the clash, flew off rather unsteadily, with a mighty beating of its wings.

Motu had saved the lamb. It was frightened but unhurt. Bleating loudly, it joined the other sheep, who took up the bleating. Jai ran up to Motu, who lay whimpering on the ground. There was no sign of the eagle. Quickly he removed his shirt and vest; then he wrapped his vest round the dog's wound, tying it in position with his belt.

Motu could not get up, and he was much too heavy for Jai to carry. Jai did not want to leave his dog alone, in case the eagle returned to attack.

He stood up, cupped his hand to his mouth, and began calling for his grandfather.

'Dada, dada!' he shouted, and presently Grandfather heard him and came stumbling down the slope. He was followed by another shepherd, and together they lifted Motu and carried him home.

Motu had a bad wound, but Grandmother cleaned it and applied a paste made of herbs. Then she laid strips of carrot over the wound—an old mountain remedy—and bandaged the leg. But it would be some time before Motu could run about again. By then it would probably be snowing and time to leave these high-altitude pastures and return to the valley. Meanwhile, the sheep had to be taken out to graze, and Grandfather decided to accompany Jai for the remaining period.

They did not see the golden eagle for two or three days, and, when they did, it was flying over the next range. Perhaps it had found some other source of food, or even another flock of sheep. 'Are you afraid of the eagle?' Grandfather asked Jai.

'I wasn't before,' said Jai. 'Not until it hurt Motu. I did

not know it could be so dangerous. But Motu hurt it too. He banged straight into it!'

'Perhaps it won't bother us again,' said Grandfather thoughtfully. 'A bird's wing is easily injured—even an eagle's.'

Jai wasn't so sure. He had seen it strike twice, and he knew that it was not afraid of anyone. Only when it learnt to fear his presence would it keep away from the flock.

The next day Grandfather did not feel well; he was feverish and kept to his bed. Motu was hobbling about gamely on three legs; the wounded leg was still very sore.

'Don't go too far with the sheep,' said Grandmother. 'Let them graze near the house.'

'But there's hardly any grass here,' said Jai.

'I don't want you wandering off while that eagle is still around.'

'Give him my stick,' said Grandfather from his bed. Grandmother took it from the corner and handed it to the boy.

It was an old stick, made of wild cherry wood, which Grandfather often carried around. The wood was strong and well-seasoned; the stick was stout and long. It reached up to Jai's shoulders.

'Don't lose it,' said Grandfather. 'It was given to me many years ago by a wandering scholar who came to the Tung temple. I was going to give it to you when you got bigger, but perhaps this is the right time for you to have it. If the eagle comes near you, swing the stick around your head. That should frighten it off!'

Clouds had gathered over the mountains, and a heavy mist hid the Tung temple. With the approach of winter, the flow of pilgrims had been reduced to a trickle. The shepherds had started leaving the lush meadows and returning to their villages at lower altitudes. Very soon the bears and the leopards and the golden eagles would have the high ranges all to themselves.

Jai used the cherry wood stick to prod the sheep along the path until they reached the steep meadows. The stick would have to be a substitute for Motu. And they seemed to respond to it more readily than they did to Motu's mad charges.

Because of the sudden cold and the prospect of snow, Grandmother had made Jai wear a rough woollen jacket and a pair of high boots bought from a Tibetan trader. He wasn't used to the boots—he wore sandals at other times—and had some difficulty in climbing quickly up and down the hillside. It was tiring work, trying to keep the flock together. The cawing of some crows warned Jai that the eagle might be around, but the mist prevented him from seeing very far.

After some time the mist lifted and Jai was able to see the temple and the snow peaks towering behind it. He saw the golden eagle, too. It was circling high overhead. Jai kept close to the flock—one eye on the eagle, one eye on the restless sheep.

Then the great bird stooped and flew lower. It circled the temple and then pretended to go away. Jai felt sure it would be back. And a few minutes later it reappeared from the other side of the mountain. It was much lower now, wings spread out and back, taloned feet to the fore, piercing eyes fixed on its target—a small lamb that had suddenly gone frisking down the slope, away from Jai and the flock.

Now it flew lower still, only a few feet off the ground, paying no attention to the boy.

It passed Jai with a great rush of air, and as it did so the boy struck out with his stick and caught the bird a glancing blow.

The eagle missed its prey, and the tiny lamb skipped away.

To Jai's amazement, the bird did not fly off. Instead it landed on the hillside and glared at the boy, as a king would glare at a humble subject who had dared to pelt him with a pebble.

The golden eagle stood almost as tall as Jai. Its wings were still outspread. Its fierce eyes seemed to be looking through and through the boy.

Jai's first instinct was to turn and run. But the cherry wood stick was still in his hands, and he felt sure there was power in it. He saw that the eagle was about to launch itself again at the lamb. Instead of running away, he ran forward, the stick raised above his head.

The eagle rose a few feet off the ground and struck out with its huge claws.

Luckily for Jai, his heavy jacket took the force of the blow. A talon ripped through the sleeve, and the sleeve fell away. At the same time the heavy stick caught the eagle across its open wing. The bird gave a shrill cry of pain and fury. Then it turned and flapped heavily away, flying unsteadily because of its injured wing.

Jai still clutched the stick because he expected the bird to return; he did not even glance at his torn jacket. But the golden eagle had alighted on a distant rock and was in no hurry to return to the attack.

Jai began driving the sheep home. The clouds had become heavy and black, and presently the first snowflakes began to fall.

Jai saw a hare go lolloping done the hill. When it was about fifty yards away, there was a rush of air from the eagle's beating wings, and Jai saw the bird approaching the hare in a sidelong drive.

'So it hasn't been badly hurt,' thought Jai, feeling a little relieved, for he could not help admiring the great bird. 'Now it has found something else to chase for its dinner.'

The hare saw the eagle and dodged about, making for a clump of junipers. Jai did not know if it was caught or not, because the snow and sleet had increased and both bird and hare were lost in the gathering snowstorm.

The sheep were bleating behind him. One of the lambs looked tired, and he stooped to pick it up. As he did so, he heard a thin, whining sound. It grew louder by the second. Before he could look up, a huge wing caught him across the shoulders and sent him sprawling. The lamb tumbled down the slope with him, into a thorny bilberry bush.

The bush saved them. Jai saw the eagle coming in again, flying low. It was another eagle! One had been vanquished, and now here was another, just as big and fearless, probably the mate of the first eagle.

Jai had lost his stick and there was no way by which he could fight the second eagle. So he crept further into the bush, holding the lamb beneath him. At the same time he began shouting at the top of his voice—both to scare the bird away and to summon help. The eagle could not easily get at them now; but the rest of the flock was exposed on the hillside. Surely the eagle would make for them.

Even as the bird circled and came back in another dive, Jai heard fierce barking. The eagle immediately swung away and rose skywards.

The barking came from Motu. Hearing Jai's shouts and sensing that something was wrong, he had come limping out of the house, ready to do battle. Behind him came another shepherd and—most wonderful of all—Grandmother herself, banging two frying-pans together. The barking, the banging and the shouting frightened the eagles away. The sheep scattered, too, and it was some time before they could all be rounded up. By then it was snowing heavily.

'Tomorrow, we must all go down to Maku,' said the shepherd.

'Yes, it's time we went,' said Grandmother. 'You can read your storybooks again, Jai.'

'I'll have my own story to tell,' said Jai.

When they reached the hut and Jai saw Grandfather, he said, 'Oh, I've forgotten your stick!'

But Motu had picked it up. Carrying it between his teeth, he brought it home and sat down with it in the open doorway. He had decided the cherry wood was good for his teeth and would have chewed it up if Grandmother hadn't taken it from him.

'Never mind,' said Grandfather, sitting up on his cot. 'It isn't the stick that matters. It's the person who holds it.'

THE WHISTLING SCHOOLBOY

From the gorge above Gangotri
Down to Kochi by the sea,
The whistling through keeps singing
That same sweet melody.

He was a whistling schoolboy once,
Who heard God Krishna's flute,
And tried to play the same sweet tune,
But touched a faulty note.

Said Krishna to the errant youth—
A bird you must become,
And you shall whistle all your days
Until your song is done.

THE LAST TRUCK RIDE

[Twice a day Pritam Singh takes his battered old truck on the narrow, mountainous roads to the limestone quarry. He is in the habit of driving fast. The brakes of his truck are in good condition. What happens when a stray mule suddenly appears on the road?]

A horn blared, shattering the silence of the mountains, and a truck came round the bend in the road. A herd of goats scattered left and right.

The goatherds cursed as a cloud of dust enveloped them, and then the truck had left them behind and was rattling along the stony, unpaved hill road.

At the wheel of the truck, stroking his grey moustache, sat Pritam Singh, a turbaned Sikh. It was his own truck. He did not allow anyone else to drive it. Every day he made two trips to the limestone quarries, carrying truckloads of limestone back to the depot at the bottom of the hill. He was paid by the trip and he was always anxious to get in two trips every day.

Sitting beside him was Nathu, his cleaner-boy. Nathu was a sturdy boy, with a round cheerful face. It was difficult to guess his age. He might have been twelve or he might have been fifteen—he did not know himself, since no one in his village had troubled to record his birthday—but the hard life he led probably made him look older than his years. He belonged to the hills, but his village was far away, on the next range.

Last year the potato crop had failed. As a result there was no money for salt, sugar, soap and flour, and Nathu's parents and small brothers and sisters couldn't live entirely on the onions and artichokes which were about the only crops that had survived the drought. There had been no rain that summer. So Nathu waved goodbye to his people and came down to the town in the valley to look for work. Someone directed him to the limestone depot. He was too young to work at the quarries, breaking stones and loading them on the trucks; but Pritam Singh, one of the older drivers, was looking for someone to clean and look after his truck. Nathu looked like a bright, strong boy, and he was brought on board at ten rupees a day.

That had been six months ago, and now Nathu was an experienced hand at looking after trucks, riding in them and even sleeping in them. He got on well with Pritam Singh, the grizzled, fifty-year-old Sikh, who had well-to-do sons in Punjab, but whose sturdy independence kept him on the road in his battered old truck.

Pritam Singh pressed hard on his horn. Now there was no one on the road—no animals, no humans—but Pritam was fond of his horn and liked blowing it. It was music to his ears.

'One more year on this road,' said Pritam. 'Then I'll sell my truck and retire.'

'Who will buy this truck? said Nathu. 'It will retire before you do.'

'Don't be cheeky, boy. She's only twenty years old. There are still a few years left in her!' And as though to prove it, he blew his horn again. Its strident sound echoed and re-echoed down the mountain gorge. A pair of wild fowl, disturbed by the noise, flew out from the bushes and glided across the road in front of the truck.

Pritam Singh's thoughts went to his dinner. 'Haven't had a good meal for days,' he grumbled.

'Haven't had a good meal for weeks,' said Nathu, although he looked quite well fed.

'Tomorrow I'll give you dinner,' said Pritam. 'Tandoori chicken and pulao.'

'I'll believe it when I see it,' said Nathu.

Pritam Singh sounded his horn again before slowing down. The road had become narrow and precipitous, and trotting ahead of them was a train of mules. As the horn blared, one mule ran forward, one ran backwards. One went uphill, one went downhill. Soon there were mules all over the place.

'You can never tell with mules,' said Pritam, after he had left them behind.

The hills were bare and dry. Much of the forest had long since disappeared. Just a few scraggy old oaks still grew on the steep hillside. This particular range was rich in limestone, and the hills were scarred by quarrying.

'Are your hills as bare as these?' asked Pritam.

'No, they have not started blasting there as yet,' said Nathu.

'We still have a few trees. And there is a walnut tree in front of our house, which gives us two baskets of walnuts every year'.

'And do you have water?'

'There is a stream at the bottom of the hill. But for the fields, we have to depend on the rainfall. And there was no rain last year.'

'It will rain soon,' said Pritam. 'I can smell rain. It is coming from the north.'

'It will settle the dust.'

The dust was everywhere. The truck was full of it. The leaves of the shrubs and the few trees were thick with it. Nathu could feel the dust near his eyelids and on his lips. As they approached the quarries, the dust increased—but it was a different kind of dust now—whiter, stinging the eyes, irritating the nostrils—limestone dust, hanging in the air.

The blasting was in progress.

Pritam Singh brought the truck to a halt. 'Let's wait a bit,' he said.

They sat in silence, staring through the windscreen at the scarred cliffs about a hundred yards down the road. There was no sign of life around them.

Suddenly, the hillside blossomed outwards, followed by a sharp crack of explosives. Earth and rock hurtled down the hillside.

Nathu watched in awe as shrubs and small trees were flung into the air. It always frightened him—not so much the sight of the rocks bursting asunder, but the trees being flung aside and destroyed. He thought of his own trees at home—the walnut, the pines—and wondered if one day they would suffer the same fate and whether the mountains would all become a desert like this particular range. No trees, no grass, no water—only the choking dust of the limestone quarries.

Pritam Singh pressed hard on his horn again to let the people at the site know he was coming. Soon they were parked outside a small shed, where the contractor and the overseer were sipping cups of tea. A short distance away some labourers were hammering at chunks of rock, breaking them up into manageable blocks. A pile of stones stood ready for loading, while the rock that had just been blasted lay scattered about the hillside.

'Come and have a cup of tea,' called out the contractor.

'Get on with the loading,' said Pritam. 'I can't hang about all afternoon. There's another trip to make and it gets dark early these days.'

But he sat down on a bench and ordered two cups of tea from the stall owner. The overseer strolled over to the group of labourers and told them to start loading. Nathu let down the grid at the back of the truck.

Nathu stood back while the men loaded the truck with limestone rocks. He was glad that he was chubby: thin people seemed to feel the cold much more—like the contractor, a skinny fellow who was shivering in his expensive overcoat.

To keep himself warm, Nathu began helping the labourers with the loading.

'Don't expect to be paid for that,' said the contractor, for whom every extra paise spent was a paisa off his profits.

'Don't worry,' said Nathu, 'I don't work for contractors. I work for Pritam Singh.'

'That's right,' called out Pritam. 'And mind what you say to Nathu—he's nobody's servant!'

It took them almost an hour to fill the truck with stones. The contractor wasn't happy until there was no space left for a single stone. Then four of the six labourers climbed on the pile of stones. They would ride back to the depot on the truck. The contractor, his overseer and the others would follow by jeep. 'Let's go!' said Pritam, getting behind the steering wheel. 'I want to be back here and then home by eight o'clock. I'm going to a wedding party tonight!'

Nathu jumped in beside him, banging his door shut. It never opened at a touch. Pritam always joked that his truck was held together with Sellotape.

He was in good spirits. He started his engine, blew his horn and burst into a song as the truck started out on the return journey.

The labourers were singing too as the truck swung round the sharp bends of the winding mountain road. Nathu was feeling quite dizzy. The door beside him rattled on its hinges.

'Not so fast,' he said.

'Oh,' said Pritam, 'And since when did you become nervous about fast driving?'

'Since today,' said Nathu.

'And what's wrong with today?'

'I don't know. It's just that kind of day, I suppose.'

'You are getting old,' said Pritam. 'That's your trouble.'

'Just wait till you get to be my age,' said Nathu.

'No more cheek,' said Pritam, and stepped on the accelerator and drove faster. As they swung round a bend, Nathu looked out of his window. All he saw was the sky above and the valley below. They were very near the edge. But it was always like that on this narrow road. After a few more hairpin bends, the road started descending steeply to the valley.

'I'll just test the brakes,' said Pritam and jammed down on them so suddenly that one of the labourers almost fell off at the back.

They called out in protest.

'Hang on!' shouted Pritam. 'You're nearly home!'

'Don't try any shortcuts,' said Nathu.

Just then a stray mule appeared in the middle of the road. Pritam swung the steering wheel over to his right; but the road turned left, and the truck went straight over the edge.

As it tipped over, hanging for a few seconds on the edge of the cliff, the labourers leapt from the back of the truck.

The truck pitched forward, bouncing over the rocks, turning over on its side and rolling over twice before coming to rest against the trunk of a scraggy old oak tree. Had it missed the tree, the truck would have plunged a few hundred feet down to the bottom of the gorge.

Two labourers sat on the hillside, stunned and badly shaken. The other two had picked themselves up and were running back to the quarry for help.

Nathu had landed in a bed of nettles. He was smarting all over, but he wasn't really hurt. His first impulse was to get up and run back with the labourers. Then he realized that Pritam was still in the truck. If he wasn't dead, he would certainly be badly injured.

Nathu skidded down the steep slope, calling out, 'Pritam, Pritam, are you all right?

There was no answer.

Then he saw Pritam's arm and half his body jutting out of the open door of the truck. It was a strange position to be in, half in and half out. When Nathu came nearer, he saw Pritam was jammed in the driver's seat, held there by the steering wheel, which was pressed hard against his chest. Nathu thought he was dead. But as he was about to turn away and clamber back up the hill, he saw Pritam open one blackened swollen eye. It looked straight up at Nathu.

'Are you alive?' whispered Nathu, terrified.

'What do you think?' muttered Pritam. He closed his eye again.

When the contractor and his men arrived, it took them almost an hour to get him to a hospital in the town. He had a broken collarbone, a dislocated shoulder and several fractured ribs. But the doctors said he was repairable—which was more than what could be said for his truck.

'The truck's finished,' said Pritam, when Nathu came to see him a few days later. 'Now 'I'll have to go home and live with my sons. But you can get work on another truck.'

'No,' said Nathu. 'I'm going home too.'

'And what will you do there?'

'I'll work on the land. It's better to grow things on the land than to blast things out of it.'

They were silent for some time.

'Do you know something?' said Pritam finally. 'But for that tree, the truck would have ended up at the bottom of the hill and I wouldn't be here, all bandaged up and talking to you. It was the tree that saved me. Remember that, boy.'

'I'll remember,' said Nathu.

SLUM CHILDREN AT PLAY

Imps of mischief,
Barefoot in the dust,
Grinning, mocking, even as
They beg you for a crust,
No angels these,
Just hungry eyes
And eager hands
To help you sympathise…
They don't want love,
They don't seek pity,
They know there's nothing
In this heartless city
But a kindred need
In those who strive
For power and pelf
Though only just alive!
They know your guilt,
They'll take your money,
And if you give too much
They'll find you funny.
Because that's what you are—
You're just a joke—
Your life is soft
And theirs all grime and smoke.

And yet they shout and sing
And do not thank your giving,
You'll fuss and fret through life
While they do all the living.

TREES BY MY WINDOW

Living at seven thousand feet, I am fortunate to have a big window that opens out on the forest so that the trees are almost within my reach. If I jumped, I could land quite neatly in the arms of an oak or horse chestnut. I have never made that leap, but the big langurs—silver-grey monkeys with long, swishing tails—often spring from the trees onto my corrugated tin roof, making enough noise to frighten all the birds away.

Standing on its own outside my window is a walnut tree, and truly this is a tree for all seasons. In winter the branches are bare, but beautifully smooth and rounded. In spring each limb produces a bright green spear of new growth, and by mid-summer the entire tree is in leaf. Toward the end of the monsoon the walnuts, encased in their green jackets, have reached maturity. When the jackets begin to split, you can see the hard brown shells of the nuts, and inside each shell is the delicious meat itself.

Every year this tree gives me a basket of walnuts. But last year the nuts were disappearing one by one, and I was at a loss as to who had been taking them. Could it have been the milkman's small son? He was an inveterate tree climber, but he was usually to be found on the oak trees, gathering fodder for his herd. He admitted that his cows had enjoyed my dahlias, which they had eaten the previous week, but he stoutly denied having fed them walnuts.

It wasn't the woodpecker either. He was out there every

day, knocking furiously against the bark of the tree, trying to pry an insect out of a narrow crack, but he was strictly non-vegetarian. As for the langurs, they ate my geraniums but did not care for the walnuts.

The nuts seemed to disappear early in the morning while I was still in bed, so one day I surprised everyone, including myself, by getting up before sunrise. I was just in time to catch the culprit climbing out of the walnut tree. She was an old woman who sometimes came to cut grass on the hillside. Her face was as wrinkled as the walnuts she so fancied, but her arms and legs were very sturdy.

'And how many walnuts did you gather today, Grandmother?' I asked.

'Just two,' she said with a giggle, offering them to me on her open palm. I accepted one, and thus encouraged, she climbed higher onto the tree and helped herself to the remaining nuts. It was impossible for me to object. I was taken with admiration for her agility. She must have been twice my age, but I knew I could never get up that tree. To the victor, the spoils!

Unlike the prized walnuts, the horse chestnuts are inedible. Even the rhesus monkeys throw them away in disgust. But the tree itself is a friendly one, especially in summer when it is in full leaf. The lightest breeze makes the leaves break into conversation, and their rustle is a cheerful sound. The spring flowers of the horse chestnut look like candelabra, and when the blossoms fall, they carpet the hillside with their pale pink petals.

Another of my favorites is the deodar. It stands erect and dignified and does not bend with the wind. In spring the new leaves, or needles, are a tender green, while during the monsoon the tiny young cones spread like blossoms in the dark green folds of the branches. The deodar enjoys the company of its own kind: where one deodar grows, there will be others. A walk in a deodar forest is awe-inspiring—surrounded on all sides by these great sentinels of the mountains, you feel as though the trees themselves are on the march.

I walk among the trees outside my window often, acknowledging their presence with a touch of my hand against their trunks. The oak has been there the longest, and the wind has bent its upper branches and twisted a few so that it looks shaggy and undistinguished. But it is a good tree for the privacy of birds. Sometimes it seems completely uninhabited until there is a whirring sound, as of a helicopter approaching, and a party of long-tailed blue magpies flies across the forest glade.

Most of the pines near my home are on the next hillside. But there is a small Himalayan blue a little way below the cottage, and sometimes I sit beneath it to listen to the wind playing softly in its branches.

When I open the window at night, there is almost always something to listen to: the mellow whistle of a pygmy owlet, or the sharp cry of a barking deer. Sometimes, if I am lucky, I see the moon coming up over the next mountain, and two distant deodars in perfect silhouette.

Some night sounds outside my window remain strange and mysterious. Perhaps they are the sounds of the trees themselves, stretching their limbs in the dark, shifting a little, flexing their fingers, whispering to one another. These great trees of the mountains, I feel they know me well, as I watch them and listen to their secrets, happy to rest my head beneath their outstretched arms.

ADVENTURES IN READING

1
Beauty in Small Books

You don't see them so often now, those tiny books and almanacs—genuine pocket books—once so popular with our parents and grandparents; much smaller than the average paperback, often smaller than the palm of the hand. With the advent of coffee-table books, new books keep growing bigger and bigger, rivalling tombstones! And one day, like Alice after drinking from the wrong bottle, they will reach the ceiling and won't have anywhere else to go. The average publisher, who apparently believes that large profits are linked to large books, must look upon these old miniatures with amusement or scorn. They were not meant for a coffee table, true. They were meant for true book lovers and readers, for they took up very little space—you could slip them into your pocket without any discomfort, either to you or to the pocket.

I have a small collection of these little books, treasured over the years. Foremost is my father's prayer book and psalter, with his name, 'Aubrey Bond, Lovedale, 1917', inscribed on the inside back cover. Lovedale is a school in the Nilgiri Hills in South India, where, as a young man, he did his teacher's training. He gave it to me soon after I went to a boarding school in Shimla in 1944, and my own name is inscribed on it in his beautiful handwriting.

Another beautiful little prayer book in my collection is called *The Finger Prayer Book*. Bound in soft leather, it is about the same length and breadth as the average middle finger. Replete with psalms, it is the complete book of common prayer and not an abridgement; a marvel of miniature book production.

Not much larger is a delicate item in calf leather, *The Humour of Charles Lamb*. It fits into my wallet and often stays there. It has a tiny portrait of the great essayist, followed by some thirty to forty extracts from his essays, such as this favourite of mine: 'Every dead man must take upon himself to be lecturing me with his odious truism, that "Such as he is now, I must shortly be". Not so shortly friend, perhaps as thou imaginest. In the meantime, I am alive. I move about. I am worth twenty of thee. Know thy betters!'

No fatalist, Lamb. He made no compromise with Father Time. He affirmed that in age we must be as glowing and tempestuous as in youth! And yet Lamb is thought to be an old-fashioned writer.

Another favourite among my 'little' books is *The Pocket Trivet, An Anthology for Optimists*, published by *The Morning Post* newspaper in 1932. But what is a trivet? The unenlightened may well ask. Well, it's a stand for a small pot or kettle, fixed securely over a grate. To be right as a trivet is to be perfectly right. Just right, like the short sayings in this book, which is further enlivened by a number of charming woodcuts based on the seventeenth century originals; such as the illustration of a moth hovering over a candle flame and below it the legend—'I seeke mine owne hurt.'

But the sayings are mostly of a cheering nature, such as Emerson's 'Hitch your wagon to a star!' or the West Indian proverb: 'Every day no Christmas, an' every day no rainy day.'

My book of trivets is a happy example of much concentrated wisdom being collected in a small space—the beauty separated from the dross. It helps me to forget the dilapidated building in which I live and to look instead at the ever-changing cloud patterns as seen from my bedroom windows. There is no end to the shapes made by the clouds, or to the stories they set off in my head. We don't have to circle the world in order to find beauty and fulfilment. After all, most of living has to happen in the mind. And, to quote one anonymous sage from my trivet, 'The world is only the size of each man's head.'

2
Written by Hand

Amongst the current fraternity of writers, I must be that very rare person—an author who actually writes by hand!

Soon after the invention of the typewriter, most editors and publishers understandably refused to look at any mansucript that was handwritten. A decade or two earlier, when Dickens and Balzac had submitted their hefty manuscrips in longhand, no one had raised any objection. Had their handwriting been awful, their manuscripts would still have been read. Fortunately for all concerned, most writers, famous or obscure, took pains over their handwriting. For some, it was an art in itself, and many of those early manuscripts are a pleasure to look at and read.

And it wasn't only authors who wrote with an elegant hand. Parents and grandparents of most of us had distinctive styles of their own. I still have my father's last letter, written to me when I was at boarding school in Shimla some fifty years ago. He used large, beautifully formed letters, and his thoughts seemed to have the same flow and clarity as his handwriting.

In his letter he advises me (then a nine-year-old) about my own handwriting: 'I wanted to write before about your writing. Ruskin... Sometimes I get letters from you in very small writing, as if you wanted to squeeze everything into one sheet of letter paper. It is not good for you or for your eyes, to get into the habit of writing too small... Try and form a larger style of handwriting—use more paper if necessary!'

I did my best to follow his advice, and I'm glad to report that after nearly forty years of the writing life, most people can still read my handwriting!

Word processors are all the rage now, and I have no objection to these mechanical aids any more than I have to my old Olympia typewriter, made in 1956 and still going strong. Although I do all my writing in longhand, I follow the conventions by typing a second draft. But I would not enjoy my writing if I had to do it straight on to a machine. It isn't just the pleasure of writing longhand. I like taking my notebooks and writing pads to odd places. This particular essay is being written on the steps of my small cottage facing Pari Tibba (Fairy Hill). Part of the reason for sitting here is that there is a new postman on this route, and I don't want him to miss me.

For a freelance writer, the postman is almost as important as a publisher. I could, of course, sit here doing nothing, but as I have pencil and paper with me, and feel like using them, I shall write until the postman comes and maybe after he has gone, too! There is really no way in which I could set up a word processor on these steps.

There are a number of favourite places where I do my writing. One is under the chestnut tree on the slope above the cottage. Word processors were not designed keeping mountain slopes in mind. But armed with a pen (or pencil) and paper, I can lie on the grass and write for hours. On one occasion, last month, I did take my typewriter into the garden, and I am still trying to extricate an acorn from under the keys, while the roller seems permanently stained yellow with some fine pollen dust from the deodar trees.

My friends keep telling me about all the wonderful things I can do with a word processor, but they haven't got around to finding me one that I can take to bed, for that is another place where I do much of my writing—especially on cold winter nights, when it is impossible to keep the cottage warm.

While the wind howls outside, and snow piles up on the windowsill, I am warm under my quilt, writing pad on my knees, ballpoint pen at the ready. And if, next day, the weather is warm and sunny, these simple aids will accompany me on a long walk, ready for instant use should I wish to record an incident, a prospect, a conversation or simply a train of thought.

When I think of the great eighteenth- and nineteenth-century writers, scratching away with their quill pens, filling hundreds of pages every month, I am amazed to find that their handwriting did not deteriorate into the sort of hieroglyphics that often make up the average doctor's prescription today. They knew they had to write legibly, if only for the sake of the typesetters.

Both Dickens and Thackeray had good, clear, flourishing styles. (Thackeray was a clever illustrator, too.) Somerset Maugham had an upright, legible hand. Churchill's neat handwriting never wavered, even when he was under stress. I like the bold, clear, straighforward hand of Abraham Lincoln; it mirrors the man. Mahatma Gandhi, another great soul who fell to the assassin's bullet, had many similarities of both handwriting and outlook.

Not everyone had a beautiful hand. King Henry VIII had an untidy scrawl, but then, he was not a man of much refinement.

Guy Fawkes, who tried to blow up the British Parliament, had a very shaky hand. With such a quiver, no wonder he failed in his attempt! Hitler's signature is ugly, as you would expect. And Napoleon's doesn't seem to know where to stop; how much like the man!

I think my father was right when he said handwriting was often the key to a man's character, and that large, well-formed letters went with an uncluttered mind. Florence Nightingale had a lovely handwriting, the hand of a caring person. And there were many like her amongst our forebears.

3
Words and Pictures

When I was a small boy, no Christmas was really complete unless my Christmas stocking contained several recent issues of my favourite comic paper. If today my friends complain that I am too voracious a reader of books, they have only these comics to blame; for they were the origin, if not of my tastes in reading, then certainly of the reading habit itself.

I like to think that my conversion to comics began at the age of five, with a comic strip on the children's page of *The Statesman*. In the late 1930s, Benji, whose head later appeared only on the Benji League badge, had a strip to himself; I don't remember his adventures very clearly, but every day (or was it once a week?) I would cut out the Benji strip and paste it into a scrapbook. Two years later, this scrapbook, bursting with the adventures of Benji, accompanied me to boarding school, where, of course, it passed through several hands before finally passing into limbo.

Of course, comics did not form the only reading matter that found its way into my Christmas stocking. Before I was eight, I had read *Peter Pan, Alice* and most of *Mr Midshipman Easy*; but I had also consumed thousands of comic papers which were, after all, slim affairs and mostly pictorial, 'certain little penny books radiant with gold and rich with bad pictures', as Leigh Hunt described the children's papers of his own time.

But though they were mostly pictorial, comics in those days did have a fair amount of reading matter, too. *The Hostspur, Wizard, Magnet* (a victim of the Second World War) and *Champion* contained stories woven round certain popular characters. In *Champion*, which I read regularly right through my prep school years, there was Rockfist Rogan, Royal Air Force (R.A.F.), a pugilist who managed to combine boxing with bombing, and Fireworks Flynn, a footballer who always scored the winning goal in the last two minutes of play.

Billy Bunter has, of course, become one of the immortals—almost a subject for literary and social historians. Quite recently, *The Times Literary Supplement* devoted its first two pages to an analysis of the Bunter stories. Eminent lawyers and doctors still look back nostalgically to the arrival of the weekly *Magnet*; they are now the principal customers for the special souvenir edition of the first issue of the *Magnet*, recently reprinted in facsimile. Bunter, 'forever young', has become a folk hero. He is seen on stage, screen and television and is even quoted in the House of Commons.

From this, I take courage. My only regret is that I did not preserve my own early comics—not because of any bibliophilic value which they might possess today, but because of my sentimental regard for early influences in art and literature.

The first venture in children's publishing, in 1774, was a comic of sorts. In that year, John Newbery brought out:

> According to Act of Parliament (neatly bound and gilt): A Little Pretty Pocket-Book, intended for the Instruction and Amusement of Little Master Tommy and Pretty Miss Polly, with an agreeable Letter to read from Jack the Giant-Killer...

The book contained pictures, rhymes and games. Newbery's characters and imaginary authors included Woglog the Giant, Tommy Trip, Giles Gingerbread, Nurse Truelove, Peregrine Puzzlebrains, Primrose Prettyface and many others with names similar to those found in the comic papers of our own century.

Newbery was also the originator of the 'Amazing Free Offer', so much a part of American comics. At the beginning of 1755, he had this to offer:

> Nurse Truelove's New Year Gift, or the Book of Books for children, adorned with Cuts and designed as a Present for every little boy who would become a great Man and ride upon a fine Horse; and to every little Girl who would become a great Woman and ride in a Lord Mayor's gilt Coach. Printed for the Author, who has ordered these books to be given gratis to all little Boys in St. Paul's churchyard, they paying for the Binding, which is only Two pence each Book.

Many of today's comics are crude and, like many television serials, violent in their appeal. But I did not know American comics until I was twelve, and by then I had become quite discriminating. Superman, Bulletman, Batman and Green Lantern, and other super heroes all left me cold. I had, by then, passed into the world of real books but the weakness for the comic strip remains. I no longer receive comics in my Christmas stocking, but I do place a few in the stockings of Gautam and Siddharth. And, needless to say, I read them right through beforehand.

DANDELION

I think it's an insult
To Nature's generosity
That many call this cheerful flower
A 'common weed'.
How dare they so degrade
A flower divinely made!
Sublimely does it bloom and seed
In sunshine or in shade,
Thriving in wind and rain,
On stony soil
On walls or steps
On strips of waste;
Tough and resilient,
Giving delight
When other flowers are out of sight,
And when its puff-ball comes to fruit
You make a wish and blow it clean away;
'Please make my wish come true,' you say,
And if you're kind and pure of heart,
Who knows? This magic flower might just respond
And help you on your way,
Good dandelion,
Be mine today.

THE DUCK IS SEVENTY

This year, ’04, I’m seventy years old,
And so is Donald Duck, I’m told.
At writing verse he’s rather slack,
I’m not much better when I quack!
So here, dear Donald, is my boast—
Roast duck is best with buttered toast.
Says Donald, ‘Friend, don’t push your luck,
You might be born again a duck!’

(For Shubhadarshini)